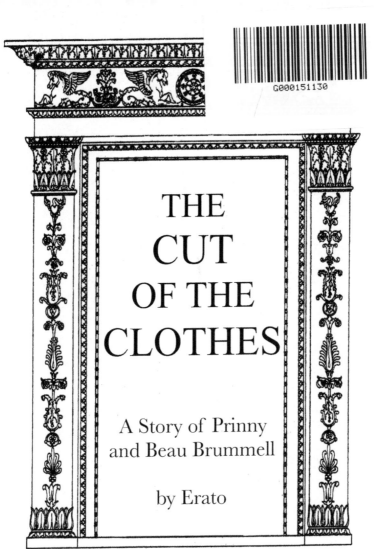

THE
CUT
OF THE
CLOTHES

A Story of Prinny
and Beau Brummell

by Erato

Alumbra Publishing

2019

Other Alumbra books by
ERATO:

Honoria

Of Crimson Joy

www.facebook.com/EratoWrites/

IV

TABLE OF CONTENTS.

All of the chapter names are taken from William Shakespeare's
Venus and Adonis.

———

VIII

CHAPTER 1.

The Weeping Morn

It would seem that an inclination to fatness runs in our Royal family. During my youth, my father provided orders to my Governor that he must restrict my diet, as a means of ensuring that my hopeless desire for overeating should not come to fit me with a gross and monstrous physique. Thus was I permitted to have pies but not their fillings; breads unbuttered; my wines watered down. My father is seen as the most beloved of Kings, and it was his comprehension, most naturally, that someday I too would be King, and it was therefore his heartfelt wish that I should be such whilst presenting an image of an *ideal*. The construction of such a favoured image was an undertaking which he had previously executed for himself: he had fashioned himself into the personage of a wise patriarch, with a large, happy family, and possessed of a contented control over his country. It was, therefore, this image that he

1

wished I should perpetuate. I should be a man that Britain, all of Europe even, could look upon with the utmost admiration. I should be a figure of perfection, with a perfect wife and family, bestowing his rulership and governance as a respectable patriarch over Church and State, and envied for his demonstrations of responsibility and care. In a word, he would have me to be Goldsmith's *Vicar of Wakefield* made flesh.

Unfortunately for my father, I loved life far too well to place such harsh restrictions upon myself. As it was once said by a great reveller: *Eheu nos miseros, quam totus homuncio nil est. Sic erimus cuncti, postquam nos auferet Orcus. Ergo vivamus, dum licet esse bene.* I heartily enjoyed life and all its attending delights. Some might have proceeded so as far as to have called me a *rake*, but these would have been but those people who did not know me. I have a heart, by God! A delicate one, at that, which is very prone to love, and all too trusting of my friends and intimates.

The love of my life was a woman named Maria Fitzherbert. I had been introduc'd to her at the Opera. She was the most covetable creature I had ever seen: graceful, lively, buxom. Her face did lack some perfection in the artistic sense, but these gentle flaws provided her with added charm. A piece called *Fountainbleau* had been play'd that night, which she had attended in the company of her cousin, Henry Errington, who was a friend of mine. I espied him after the shew, when he was waiting for his carriage, and I ventured to greet him. Naturally, I also inquired about the pretty girl he had on his arm, and so were we introduced: Mrs. Fitzherbert and the Prince of Wales.

In my life, I had access to any pretty young girl under creation, but such simple beauties never struck my senses. Maria was *sur toutes choses*. I regarded her as an utter Venus, in all her aspects. She was six years my elder, and widowed twice over, but I wanted her more than any other thing in the world. As for myself, I was discover'd to her at my own acme: I was handsome, portly but not yet fat, three and twenty years old, and fill'd with the characteristics of youth and vigor. I was heir apparent to the throne, and my father's illness was not yet manifest in any condition that humiliated me. I had every reason to expect Maria should be pleased by my courtship, and by my attentions.

Some days after our most fortuitous meeting, I saw her at a ball, and I danced with her as often as she could be prevailed upon to accept me. I began to learn who were her friends, and once knowing this, I made it my business to secure invitations to all the same dinners and dances which she attended: after each, I would beg her to grant me the honor of seeing her home in my carriage. I sent her gifts; I called upon her to excess; I pledg'd to her my eternal love. My heart beat for none but her. Yet it was apparent that even my utmost affection and obedience to her, was not enough to satisfy, for she would not grant me her hand when I begged her to marry me; and I can assure you that I made these proposals to marry her very very very often. It is true, that it was entirely illegal for us to wed, for she was Catholic; and some stupid century-old law forbade any one who had married a Catholic from sitting upon the throne. Moreover, I was not consider'd to have my majority in this instance, and in consequence, I could not wed without the permission of my Royal father. It was quite certain that this permission was a thing that he would never grant, in consideration of the aforementioned matter of Maria's religion. Notwithstanding this, I loved her, and I would do any thing to gain her love. My life was but an agony without her: I cried myself to sleep at night, I loved her so. By day I sighed, groaned, and could not concentrate on any task, be it diversion or duty. I obsessed over her. I curs'd the world, that fate should have kept us apart over such silly causes as an outdated prejudice. Nothing could be enjoyed by me without Maria's love bestow'd to me. I needed love if I were to live, for why should I even exist if I could not be beloved?

I wanted her for my wife. I had kept mistresses before this time, but I had never known such feelings for them as those which I suffered for Maria. I propos'd to her each and every time I saw her, tho' being refused at each, with she ever citing that her acceptance was impossible, for it would be high treason were she to accept me. I persisted all the same. At last, in a desperate effort to evade my attentions, Maria made an attempt to flee across the channel, to Europe, where I held not power or influence, and could not follow her. I cou'd not bear the thought of being without her, the idea that life would have to proceed so emptily! My heart was shattered. I cou'd not go on living. I took a knife and stabbed myself in the heart — or rather, aiming for my heart, but too drunk to hit my mark. Still, I bled, and after I was wrestled down and forced into sick-bed, I made earnest threats that I would pull off my bandages and tear the wound back open if Maria would not return herself to me. My friends tracked her down and escorted her to her devoted lover's bedside. I wept and begged for her to marry me. I proclaimed that I should die without her, and at so long last, she was *prevailed upon to grant me her hand.* We embraced, with tears in our eyes: we drew up a marriage contract at that very moment, and when I was well enough, we were married in secret.

Naturally, this marriage was never regarded as legal; but she, I, and all of London understood that she was as good as my wife. I had won the love which I had sought.

Yet, though I have never, no, never never ceas'd to love her, I will own that I have not always been constant towards her. It is our duty, as men, to win love; but it is the duty of women to maintain it. I have had my portion of mistresses; perhaps more than my fair portion; and beyond that, there was the not insignificant matter of my *arranged marriage*, this being the one which is regarded as official and legally binding.

It was the members of the Court that had set about choosing for me what bride they thought was best. My mistress at the time was Frances, Lady Jersey: she took it upon herself to ensure that the woman *she* especially wish'd to see me wed, would be the one selected. Her recommendation was that it be my German cousin Caroline: a woman that she knew, from the beginning, I should absolutely detest. This she did, because she did not wish to provide herself with a rival. Caroline was thus selected as the best choice for me to marry, because she was the worst; and I was so smitten with Frances that I did not question her judgment, at that time. It really was of little consequence, for in effect, it did not matter who had been *chosen* for me, as it was still upon me to actually consent to be married. Sadly for myself, a misfortune took place which compelled me to bestow that consent.

One must understand: in the year 1788 there had been a crisis. My father, whose mind had always been somewhat delicate, went completely out of his senses. He would speak for hours upon hours about what can only be described as *nothing*, unpausing and unstoppable in his words. By the time that he had done, he wou'd be foaming at the mouth. Sometimes he wou'd convulse, and his courtiers wou'd be forc'd to sit upon him, as their only means to hold him down. It became necessary that he be sent away from the Court in London, in order to recover himself. But in the meantime, who was to rule the country? This duty, it seemed most natural, should fall to me. I was the heir apparent, and surely would someday become the King. Yet there was reluctance from the government to allow for this transition of power, for I was very much dislik'd by the men in Parliament, who would have to approve the bestowing of such powers unto me. I suppose I can understand the cause of their prejudice: the skirt-chasing, horse-racing, hard-drinking, wed-to-a-Catholic *Prinny*, made Regent of Great Britain? They were appalled by the very thought. The point ultimately became moot, for my father was able to recover his health before any decision could go through, one way or another; but the entire episode left me entirely dismay'd. I observ'd that my conduct was not so different from that displayed by many others, who held like positions, both in past and in present. Why was I thought so exceptionally unfit to rule? What was it about me, especially, that rendered me so *despised*?

This necessitated a resolution from me, that from that time forward, I should look to be a man that all the world should love, and that any body in the world could be proud to call *their own King*. Therefore, I set about to creating, for myself, a presentation, a pageantry: an image of a beautiful, princely fellow to adore. I had my pictures painted by the best artists, for which I dressed in clothes which were calculated to depict me as a strong and attractive. I obsessed about the appearance of my military regiments, and I adjusted and improved their garments with the greatest alacrity, so that they would display a glorious reflection of my good taste. Yet, as I went about all of these tasks, I spent my way into some considerable debt: my yearly allowance was not adequate to pay for the expenses I incurred, for evidently my ideas were a good deal bigger than my income. Reduc'd to this shameful situation, an offer was made to me: if I would marry the woman who had been chosen for me, I would be granted the reward of seeing my debts all abolish'd. With every eye in the world upon me, the moneylenders were not going to front me any thing further unless I settled this matter; and my artisans and tradesmen were no longer eager to wait upon me unless I could pay their bills. Thus the Ministers had me by the hip: I certainly did not see any better way I could have every thing repaid, and so, I agreed to the terms, unsavory as I felt them to be.

I was not alone in finding the arrangement disagreeable: Maria was not the least bit happy to abide it. For me to take on a mistress was one thing, but she was not willing to stomach another wife to stand in her place. She declared that, if I would follow through with this marriage, that our relationship was *finita*, and she returned to me all the little gifts and tokens of affection which I had given to her in our ten years' time together. From there, she refused my visits and was deaf to every one of my ceaseless lamentations. Such use, such cruel and monstrous use, left me devastated. I grew so weak and pale that one would have scarcely known me. As a matter of fact, I may have never looked more handsome.

On the day of my compelled marriage to Caroline, I was attended by a young gentleman I had only recently become a good friend to. His name was *George Brummell*. This young man was a Cornet in one of my regiments, and not yet out of his teen years. On that unhappy morning, I had locked myself in my closet, and I admitted no entry to any body. I was finding myself to be very badly afflicted by the inward agonies of reservations and second thoughts, with regard to what I was about to undertake, by this marriage. I wept, whilst I suck'd down a bottle of champagne, and considered with frantick desperation whether there were any means by which I could extricate myself from this most wretched quandary. I gazed at Maria's beautiful portrait, which was engraved into a gem that dangled from a ribband about my neck, and I wept at the memories of her, and I so wished that I could undo what I was finding myself forc'd to undertake. My friends and servants rapped frantically upon the door, and call'd to me from without, with aim to coax me into opening for them so I might prepare for the miserable ceremony, that was to destroy my life in ways I could not yet foresee. At length a somewhat drawling voice came through, which I knew to belong to the young Cornet who was to attend me on this day:

"Aw, your Highness, how can you be upset when you have a suit like this to wear?"

My wedding suit, of black and gray satin, bedecked with silver lace and spangles, was awaiting me through the door. I had tried it once before, at the fitting. It truly was a stunning creation: a perfect marriage of glitter and refinement. I had fretted for hours over its design, and had spent a small fortune upon it.

"You know it is too decadent to wear to the races, Prinny," the youth continued, affectionately calling me by my nickname. "Come, let us see you in it."

Despondent as I was for the circumstance which had engendered the suit's creation, I had been, indeed, looking with great pleasure to wearing it. Grudgingly, I opened the door. My doing so provoked an audible sigh of relief from every body without.

My day-old face powder was left in streaks down my cheeks, from the way I had been weeping; surely I looked dreadful. Brummell, dressed in his uniform of the 10th Hussars, sought to comfort me with sympathy and reassurance, whilst my valets tied and pinned me into the elaborate ensemble of fabric and lace that made up this most elaborate shroud for what may as well have been my funeral.

"It is a monstrous thing they make me do," I said to Brummell. "Yet I must abide it. It is a sad thing to be a Prince."

"Yet Princes are envied," he answered me. "You agreed to the match yourself, did you not? Aw, surely you do not doubt yourself now! Perhaps you will *like* her, once you meet her." Suddenly his eye was caught by some thing, and he directed his words to the valets: "Sir, take care to press the back of the waistcoat as you tie it. Otherwise it forms a bulge."

The valets adjusted me as instructed. I thanked Brummell for his care: this remarkable attention to detail, which he alone seem'd to possess, was the reason I had sought to have him attend me on that day. The wedding was for shew as much as for any thing, so it was a shew we were necessitated to put on. I therefore had to be stageworthy, and truly I was excited for the opportunity to be a spectacle, even if I detested the conditions it was to be under.

Once I was dressed in all my finery of gems, ribbands and red-heeled shoes, my face was repainted and powder'd, and my wig was plac'd, I made my way downstairs to meet, for the first time, the woman whom I was to marry. Lord Malmesbury, who had been looking after Caroline since her arrival in England, was given the honorable position of introducing us. She came forward, dressed in a fashionable white gown of gauzy material, heavily ornamented. She made an attempt to kneel before me, and I raised her up: this was all perfect etiquette. We compelled smiles of friendship to one another, and I took her by the hand.

"Madam, it is an honor to meet you, at last," I said most regally.

"You are fatter than your picture," was her utterly unbelievable reply to me. I need hardly say that I was taken aback, and was very deeply discomfited by that ill-mannered response. Her English was decently adept, though heavily accented toward her native German. I considered whether or not German, or even French, might be a more comfortable tongue for us to continue with, for it might at least reduce my humiliation before the courtiers, several of whom were already snickering at her tactless remarks.

As we proceeded through the hall, Brummell hastened his pace to meet with me, and spoke into my ear:

"Do not pay her too much heed. She is from a very backwards country; why it seems that the Germans have not even discover'd soap."

It was true, her odor was certainly that of the animal variety rather than of floral perfume or scented washballs. I shall state, that this realization was of no comfort to me. I sent Lord Malmesbury to bring me some brandy, posthaste.

Thus the German cow and I endured the disgraceful ceremony of marriage together. Our wedding portrait was painted by Henry Singleton: it well depicts the looks of irritation and and dismay upon our faces as I and Caroline were pledg'd to one another. As I stood at her side, I swear that her gutter-like odor grew more and more pronounced. She must have been sweating. By the time that the wedding feast was upon us, I had scarcely any appetite with which to eat it. As Caroline sat beside me, conversing with the guests at the table, which included my own parents, and many other members of my family, she kept making mortifyingly obscene jokes in French, and inquiring of me as to why I did not eat. "You are so large, how did you become so without eating?"

I found myself to have little desire for food, but I gulped down brandy as swift as I was able, whilst listening to my new bride's humiliating efforts at chit-chat. The liquor had a most pleasing effect upon me, and I was enabled at least to talk to some of my family at the table. My brother Frederick and his wife Frederica (Duke and Duchess of York) were near to me, and in my stupor I began to beg them to hurry to produce an heir to the throne. "My God, can you really expect it from me and this creature? She, to be the mother of a future King?" They only smiled pacifically and assured me that every thing would turn out well, the both of them forcing a false and polite optimism in answer to my utmost despair and grief.

By the time that Caroline and I retired for bed, for the necessities of the wedding night, my world appear'd to me in a dim and choppy view, like would be seen through the spokes of a turning wheel. I was ill and intoxicated from too much brandy, and I ardently wished for nothing more than to sleep, but I had duties to perform. To my dismay, they involved stripping out of my lovely suit (which had made up the only pleasant part of my day) and settling into the sheets with my new bride.

She was less experienc'd than I, certainly (for I was a married man already); but I hoped that I might at least derive some pleasure from introducing her to the marital act. She was, however, even less enthused for it than myself.

"Is that the full extent of it?" she ask'd, as she examined me indelicately. "I shall have to draw my legs well back."

I was dismayed, and nearly lost my spirit altogether. The remark suggested that she might not be so inexperienced as I had been led to believe: they had said to me that she had never even danced with another man before me, but evidently she was kept quite inform'd of some other physical matters thro' some mechanism. Notwithstanding her concern, I breached her gates without difficulty. I held my face down, close to myself, allowing the perfume of my own Cologne water to disguise the unwashed odor of the creature below me; by God, she smelled as if she had been rolling in a gutter outside of an *abattoir* whilst eating raw onions. My floral perfume could conceal it somewhat, and I made every endeavor to imagine some more desirable being in her place; but my illusions were shattered when the harpy spoke to me once again:

"You know, it is not so bad. Even if you do not smile at me, your chins do so." I think she may have been endeavoring to make light of the situation with a joke, but all she succeeded at was to render me limp with discomfiture, forcing me to halt my task. I begged her for a few minutes' peace, so I might rest and recuperate. I could not tell whether she was disappointed by this; I was, for my part, less disappointed than humiliated. That I should be subject to such degradation, for the sake of money! I cringed when I considered it; but I needed simply to have done with this, to fulfill my duties, to plant some Royal seed in her, and I could then be done with all of it and find myself a debt-free Prinny once more.

"Very well," sneered our Royal hero, with a sort of arrogance racing up to mask his sensations of guilt and inadequacy. "There are dozens of other women in this country who find my physical characteristics adequate in all regards. It must be some thing quite the matter with you, that hinders me."

"You leave me parched as a piece of toast," whined Caroline in turn. Good heavens, what a revolting simile! I could not eat toast again for months thereafter.

"Think of someone else, then," I groaned. "God knows I shall be obliged to." We were well past any hope of politeness by now, between us.

"I shall think of the little soldier that followed you about to-day," said she. I suspect that she had hop'd to wound me with her announced choice. "You can think of him, too. It might help you."

I was infuriated by her implication, but out of pride I mounted her once more and suffered through the most unpleasant bout of copulation that I have ever known in my life. I was nearly in tears by the end of it. When done, I withdrew myself from the bed. Being a gentleman, I let her have it to herself, whereas I lodged myself upon the floor by the fireside. Dressed in my nightshirt, I spread out in that spot, and passed from that living nightmare into a more otherworldly one.

In the morning, Caroline and I mutually agreed that we found one another to be utterly unbearable. We made an accord that from that moment forward, our only common goal would be to never see one another ever again. My duty to marry her was fulfill'd. I had consummated the union, so what more did we need?

After I had retreated to my closet, I saw Cornet Brummell again. Naturally, I conveyed nothing to him of the horrors which I had experienced on the previous night; but I did especially want his advice on a certain matter which had come to provoke an additional upset to my tranquility.

"Brummell," said I, striving to conceal how shaken I was by the whole velitation I had lately endured. "Do you suppose that there is any cut of clothing which will cause me to look more slender?" Brummell was always the best dressed man in a room: even when forced into a uniform, he always wore it neater than any one else. He was my sage of fashion, a veritable prophet of what was or was not becoming in clothes.

"A cut?" he repeated after me, in that innocent, friendly tone that he always took with me. "Aw, no, that might be too great a demand upon the skills of a tailor... however..." He seemed hesitant to make his suggestion, and lowered his voice before daring to articulate it: "Have you considered the work of a *corsetier*?"

The idea was a brilliant one. I made immediate arrangements for a fitting at the finest one in the city. Within a few weeks, I was in possession of my *belt*, as we discreetly called it: my shape was instantly transformed to a more youthful, slender figure by the help of that device, altho' it took some determination, and the help of three servants, to get me into it.

This was the first great innovation of fashion which I ow'd to Mr. Brummell, and there were to be countless more to come. The youth had a great genius when it came to any thing made from cloth, and I was glad to have bestowed him with my patronage. He was, I reckon'd, a most helpful tool towards my wonderful goal of setting the fashion of the world. My marriage restored my financial powers to me, and the time was ripe to reinvent myself as the master and mode-maker of Europe. Brummell was there to help me, and in return I was to help him towards the achievement of his goals for status and wealth within society, as I shall hereafter explain.

CHAPTER 2.

The Field's chief Flower

"A filthy cravat will degrade the whole of one's look. Why bother to wear it at all, if one will wear it in such condition? The function of it is to improve and to decorate one's costume. Do these men truly think a filthy dishrag draped about the neck achieves the same effect? Gentlemen: have some pride and wear a clean one, for the love of God! Keep the poor bleach-maids in some comfort." That was some thing Brummell once said. Items fashioned of white cloth are the most difficult to keep clean, but clean they had to be. A spot or smudge gave immediate cause to return it to the washerwoman, in his view. I must suppose that it was for this reason, that he tended to prefer dark, sad hues for all suits, as these will mimick cleanliness for longer spans. Nothing was more dismaying to his eye than a jolly rose or peacock blue or leaf green jacket, all browned at the sleeves and hems, with grease stains shewing across the front. Yet such a sight amongst our noblemen was not so uncommon, at one time: *deshabille* had become the mode, and we loved our bright hued jackets and waistcoats against our pale-powdered hair, despite how unforgivingly they betrayed even meager traces of dirt.

The first time that I encountered Mr. Brummell, he was aged about fifteen years. It was on the Terrace at Windsor Castle. He was in the shadow of the grand old structure, dressed in his school uniform from Eton, the view below us so splendid. Yet contrary to the intentions of his fellow classmates, he was there to see not the prospect below, but the fashions of the moment as worn by those other men and women that adorned the enclave. What were his betters all wearing? This was a matter of some importance to him, for he had fast found that, in a world where he was inferior in status to many of his schoolmates, his tiny improvements to the standard were what fixed upon him a power to be situated apart and above all the rest. He told me, years later, that after he took to wearing his famous gold buckle on his uniform's cravat, a boy who formerly had teazed and insulted him, actually became complimentary and even friendly towards him. Indeed, in a world where all had to dress as one, he found he could stand out favourably by dressing more cleanly and with greater care than the others. But I am forgetting myself: it was on the Terrace at Windsor, where he had gone to see the fashions of the promenaders, that he was to receive the unexpected treat of seeing the Prince himself to emerge; for, back then, that was an event for Mr. Brummell. When I emerg'd, I fixed my eyes upon him and smiled, then bid my companions to approach him. I did this very casually, and he was perhaps too young to fully recognize that this was not some thing that every young man could expect to have take place in his life. I still wore floral embroideries and hair powder, in those days: he was clothed in his simple little school uniform, but it was so crisp, clean and tailored that I said to him, "What a charming young man! Why, you look as if you could be sitting for a portrait. Do you always dress up so nicely?"

He answered to me that, indeed, such care for neatness was always his habit. I offered up a few more quick and complimentary words, before proceeding away with my companions to whatever business I was about on that afternoon, thus leaving young George Brummell to stand where he had been. He later said to me that he was left vibrating with a kind of warmth from these attentions: for it was an indescribable compliment to him that even Princes admired his clothing. You can be assured that he told every one at the school of the adventure; being cautious, of course, not to seem as if he bragged about it; and at those times when his relation of the event crossed too deeply into that realm, he endeavor'd to make jokes and humor enough to compensate for the bad manners of it, for humor is to the mind what beauty is to the eye. It amends for much.

His father had been of a man of lowish station, but positioned right at the cusp, where he could see better views for his boy. In consequence, young Brummell was sent to Eton, with the promise that *rex eris si recte feceris*. From there, like any King over his Court, it was he that set the fashions. I would not say that he was a poor student, and I am of understanding that he was never flogged for any misbehavior; but I suppose he cared less for his studies than he did for making friends and forming attachments, and in truth that *was* the purpose for which his father had sent him to the school, so in that regard he fulfilled his project admirably. Brummell wished for every body to like him, and for the most part, he was capable to achieve this aim. He was witty enough for a schoolboy, and compassionate: there is a story told of how he rescued a simple-minded boatman from the abuses of a group of his schoolmates, who had undertaken a prankish design to throw the poor fellow from a low bridge. So, kindness was not beyond him, even if he did have a critical eye and a tendency for cattish behavior. His attention to fashion and manners earned him the nickname of "Buck" (being, at that time, a term for an admirable follower of fashion.)

From Eton he went on to Oxford, though certainly not with any intention to enter the clergy as is often the case for those who attend there. No, it was to make more friends, and to learn just enough to fit into their society: the *ton*, as we said in those days. What he came to understand was that in the *ton*, it was *tout entièrement* to *be seen with favour*. He did not have the funds to dress in finer silks or newer fashions (yet), but d--- me if he was not more splendid than any Duke. The fact was that, at Oxford, he kept the laundress very busy (and please do not read some lewd implication into that declaration, I mean but to say that he never wore a shirt, cravat or stockings twice, unless they had been cleaned in the meantime.) White shews any thing and every thing. He would send the gyp each evening to deliver what things he had worn that day, for washing. He may have spent more for laundry than for food. Yet again, his example came to be followed: soon one never witnessed any student to dress in nappy cotton stockings or dingy cravats. He had become the master of all things sartorial, and there was some thing about him, some kind of admirable sparkle in his personality and manners, which instilled in every person the earnest wish to follow him, to imitate him, to do whatever he did. Every body at that school look'd to him to set the mode, and navigated whatever course he would chart. That was a big responsibility for him at sixteen, to be sure; but still he did his utmost to gratify the expectations which were upon him. The most important thing he did on any day, was to decide what he should wear. He sometimes had to beg his father for more money to buy the clothes which fixed him with his newfound status, but on these occasions he merely assured old Mr. Brummell of the great effect it was producing upon his society, at which the old man would relent, and let his son have whatever he needed for the continuation of his project.

Yet it was not for long that he had necessity to carry on in this manner: Brummell was still only sixteen when his father died. Altho' his father's station in life was not high, that is not to suggest that the family was by any means poor, and he receiv'd about one third of the total estate, this amounting to a little less than £65,000 for himself to do with, more or less, as he pleased; notwithstanding that, awaiting his coming of age, it was to be subject to the command of his guardian Sir John Macpherson.

As he had really only been in school to please his father, he withdrew almost immediately upon that man's death, and it was then for himself to find a career that would prove to befit a gentleman of his pretensions. By necessity, that amounted to a choice of occupation in the clergy, the law, politics, or the military. He chose the one that required no further education. He put down a portion of the money which he had receiv'd (about £735, as I recall) to buy himself the position of a Cornet in one of the finest regiments in the realm: the 10th Hussars.

He confided in me at a later time, that he had selected them for the reason that they had "the most attractive uniforms, and so many lovely variations for different purposes: always tight leggings in spotless white, and plenty of metal braid." Beyond these visible benefits, the 10th Hussars were the Prince's Own, and Brummell speculated on whether he might be able to impress himself upon me a second time, for, apart from my Royal father, I was in every effect the highest ranking man in the country. This is not to suggest Brummell's other companions in the Hussars were poor alliances, not at all. Several others of rank and family were made his brothers in arms, and he was secured many profitable introductions through them. But his Prinny was the prize: it was my attention he should have to catch, if he would ease his way into society. It was lucky for him that I was well known to have a strong predilection for companions who had some marked peculiarity of character about them, and when one is already the highest ranking person in the land, I suppose one can always afford to lower one's standards for the sake of fellowship (indeed, where else can one go, but lower?)

I was, at this time, undertaking the promotion of a new mode for a very high collar. This was done by me, in order to conceal my own development of multiple chins, and to compel myself to hold high my head, that I might slenderize my neck somewhat; and also to compel the instantaneous beautification which a fine posture provides. Yet for all that I loved clothes, alas! I loved food just as well; and my fine chefs and scientifically designed kitchens were wreaking havoc upon the shape of my poor, helpless figure. My ploy to conceal the developing ruffle of neck-flesh, by this new mode, was a success; and indeed, on a man of slighter figure its effect was shewn to be all the more striking. The clothes of the Hussars were to be re-edified so to include this innovation. I went myself to shew it to the men, and to demonstrate how the stiffened collar was employ'd to hold the throat in place. It was through this exercise that Brummell and I came again into contact, and he, with all the bravery of a boy of sixteen to a man twice his age, reminded me of our previous meeting. He was fortunate, for, if I did not remember him, I at least feigned that I did; and whatever magnetism he had produced upon me the first time we had met, yet remained in his power. We soon became greater than military brothers: we became close friends. Our union was a Godsend. The great spirit of Beauty desired nothing more than to see London, the greatest city in the world, beautifi'd to its utmost: and it seemed that we two had been designated to serve as her sacred Ministers. Together, he and I would undertake the challenge of seeing the city aglow with the new era of fashion. The old center of all things sartorial, Paris, was at that time in a state of disaster: after the Revolution, the

French *incroyables* were wearing any thing they could think of, with perfectly ludicrous results: blue and green wigs, prancing about barefoot, pierced ears on men and women alike, tunics *sans-culottes*. The one constant was the admiration for the ancient Greeks: every one in the world endeavor'd to follow their venerable example, though, naturally, whilst utilizing the new discoveries that were made in the few centuries since. The primary attraction concerning Greek fashion was its *simplicity*. The women of the world were already discovering the advantages of these charming and uncomplicated fashions; they had left off their hip bolsters and hoops for an easier mode which better displayed the beauty of the figure; which is really what one's clothing should emphasize, and strive to flatter. The question was, could the *macaroni* fashions of the Englishmen be cast away, to be replaced with some thing of a like simplicity? It was the duty of Brummell and myself to attempt it.

Brummell retired from the Hussars at the age of eighteen, despite my effort to retain him by granting him a promotion to the rank of Captain. By that time he reported so rarely for duty that he was but little miss'd. He really was in no need of such a job: he was Prinny's close friend and companion. In those days, no higher position in the realm could be attained, or hoped for. By the time that he was one and twenty, his *nomme de guerre* had gone from *Buck* to *Beau*.

It is a French word, meaning *fine* or *handsome*. There had been but a few before him worthy of that epithet: Beau Nash, in Bath, who made that city the social center that it is; and Beau Fielding, the great seducer under Charles II. It strikes me that it was normally a nickname given unto men whose Christian name was *Robert*, as in both the examples provided; but George Brummell defied every thing common. He was a beau, he was the apex of a beau, he was *beau ideal*. His figure was handsome, and reported to be the finest in all of England. His clothing was spotless, the cut and stitch of his suits was without equal, his choice of fabrics was always strikingly understated but pleasing to the eye. His obsession for cleanliness surpassed the condition of his linens: his body, too, he cleaned most impeccably. I was often so fascinated with his procedure that I would go to his home in Chesterfield Street to observe his morning toil and moil.

Upon entering his closet, he first brushed his teeth (a rare thing at the time, though which since has been made much more commonplace, by his influence.) With a silver tooth-brush dipped in powder, he scrubb'd them smooth and white. He would spit, from time to time, into a silver basin: clay was not clean enough to spit into, he was known to have said. When he had completed this task, his breath would have upon it the faintest perfume of orris root, this being a key ingredient in his choice of tooth powder: and this was the entire extent of his perfumery.

The second task for him to undertake, was to shave his face. Hot water would be brought by his man, with which he would soak a cloth, and this he used to moisten his beard before commencing. He would whip up some shaving soap and lather his face in the traditional manner, and I suppose his method of scraping his face was not in any significant way different from what any other man would do in the same circumstance. At the end of his operation, he would wipe up any remaining soap from his face or hair (which hair he wore, at this time, in imitation of my own Brutus cut.)

After this he would produce a pair of tweezers, and with a small mirror to aid him, he inspected his face for any barbs of beard or other unwanted sproutings about his eyebrows or nose which had been overlook'd, and would pluck them away. His face had to be like a marble statue, free from all imperfection.

After this was the great event: the solid two hours of bathing. Sometimes he took longer, though I think that might only be from the interruptions of his visitors who came to watch him at it with all the fascination of David looking upon Bathsheba; but do not suppose, as certain lewd women have suggested, that there was anything amiss in it. Every man in the city envied his physique, and marveled at how carefully and intensively he washed it. The Beau preferred hot water for his bathing, which he would have brought up to his closet by two servants. Then he wou'd crouch into the basin with a brush and a bar of the finest Castile soap. He would begin by scrubbing his fingertips and nails, removing any trace of grime or rough skin; then proceeding to his hands, then arms, and so forth. He scoured at each section of his skin till it was red, then mov'd to the next. Nothing was neglected, from his ears to his toes. He emerged from his ablutions smelling only faintly of the sweet, dry scent of plain Castile, and he added no further perfume or powder above this.

He often entreated me to adopt a similar regimen for myself: "You would not need to use those perfumes, and go about smelling like the gardener raked you up at Kew, if you would simply clean yourself with some care."

"And why," said I, "should I spend hours in cleaning myself, when ten minutes and a dash of perfume achieves as good of an effect?"

"You are impossible, Prinny," he said with a toss of his head.

The truth was that I had made some attempts towards the emulation of his skin-roughening regimen, for myself. I scrubbed my body for as long as I could bear it; I soaked myself in steaming water. The whole procedure took too long for too little reward, for my taste; the only real difference that I saw, was that it caused my skin to sting, wither and start peeling away. Yet it was no hindrance to my fascination that *he* could bear it each day.

"You may have the whole day to spend in cleaning yourself," said I, defending my pride, "but some of us men have duties to attend, beyond just the gaming table." To my knowledge, the inheritance he receiv'd from his father, and the favours of Dame Fortune at the card table, were his only sources of funds for his lavish lifestyle; though I, or some other wealthy friend, might from time to time make a little gift to him to help him on his way.

"I've too much time stored up to waste it all upon some thing so mindless as work," said he. "It is *so* ungentlemanly to work."

This was truth, but a truth which few gentlemen could live out whilst simultaneously paying for the other pleasures of gentlemanhood. The goal was ideally to find an occupation which left one with as little to do as possible: land ownership was the favourite. I myself had an income fixed upon me by Parliament and my Royal father, and from time to time, if it proved inadequate for my needs, I might find it necessary to ask for a little more. Nevertheless, I was expected to apply that money to things beyond only myself: arts, musick, buildings, and those things which would beautify and glorify our fair country were also under my care. I did my part in that, for certain. It was utterly my duty to make sure that Great Britain was shewn to be a land of perfect loveliness, which would sparkle above any other country on this earth. The government, for the time being, was for my father to operate: for my part, I was to attend to the spirit of the land. Thus I strove to set an example: my followers were known as the *Corinthians*, and Brummell was one amongst them. We decided upon our era's fashions for the cut of the clothes, the trim of the hair, and for the admirable pass-times. Snuff was one that had been decided upon as a favourite occupation: I held no love for the substance itself, but I could well admire the art in the ritual of taking *un pris*. Therefore I would have special blends of tobacco prepared for me, and from innumerable little boxes that existed to shew off art for art's own sake, I would take a pinch, and deliberately drop the powder well before it could graze my nostril. The glamour of the box, the hand-dance in taking up the snuff, the excuse to display a fine finger-ring or two: that was the provision of snuff-taking. It was all about the spectacle; there was no substance behind it. Maybe a bit like Brummell himself.

In those days, I lived only for fashion. Each morning I would be strung into my restricting garment by my valet, then fitted with the remainder of my well-made clothes, all designed by the finest tailors in the country. I had, in my closet, three full-length mirrors, arranged in a sort of triangle, so I could see front, side and back: I would not let any one have an unflattering view of me. By these means was I transformed, every day, into the most handsome man in all the land: "The first gentleman of Europe" as I was known. I had made no meager or easy endeavors to gain that status, but gain it I did. I was the trend-setter. I was the master of the mode. I had to be: how I was looked upon was all that was valued in me. I am but a fat son of a madman, if you strip me of the clothes (and even that madman has never looked too kindly upon me); but decked out, a transformation took place, and I was *someone* to admire. It was therefore utterly vital, for my own sake, that I dress in clothing fit for a Prince, for in that weave of threads was the seat of all the respect and admiration I was due.

I suppose, in effect, this was a similitude between myself and Beau Brummell. He was nothing but his clothes, too: a boy from an obscure family, tolerable fortune but nothing remarkable in a city like London, a pleasant face but not the most comely one ever saw. His good looks were acquired, not God-given. Thus we worked our influence upon each other, he imitating me and I him, improving ourselves through the wits and arts of two great minds, instead of just one.

CHAPTER 3.

A War of Looks

While my marriage to Maria Fitzherbert was not regarded as legal or binding in England, the Pope had acknowledged it as a genuine union. Maria and I, too, thought of it as a true marriage: and even if we might have split, such a situation was not unheard of in true and genuine marriages. There were many spouses of the *ton* who rarely conversed with one another: in fact I mined many of my mistresses from those very ranks, and such was effectively my situation with my Princess, Caroline. Just because she had cast me off, Maria could not be thought entirely free from me. Her own reputation required her to acknowledge herself as still my wife; and as for myself, it was not as if I had ceased in any way to love her. Far from it! I was heartbroken when she had declared a termination to our *amours*. When it at last became apparent that Caroline and I would not be living as husband and wife in

34

any meaningful fashion, I wrote to Maria and told her every thing which had transpired, and proclaim'd to her all of my love still retained for her. She replied (oh, thank heavens, she *replied!*) but it was only with a frosty sort of friendship. Still, I had prevailed upon her once before through such embarrassments, and I meant to succeed with her again. Unfortunately I was not the handsome young creature that had won her heart the first time around. More than a decade and a half had since made its mark upon me, and that was compounded to those flaws from which I have for ever suffered. I have not been blessed with a fair and licked-over complexion, even if the portrait artists might depict me so. No: my skin is ruddy and bright, and not merely on the cheeks where such a trait might be desirous, but rather it is all over red, as if I were perpetually sunburnt. Nose, chin, forehead: all are confoundedly red. I often use white powder, fashioned of bismuth and chalk, to fade the too-bright hue and bring my face to a more becoming shade. Unfortunately, this mask demands that repairs be made several times each day, and if I should find myself to sweat, or to weep, or even to simply be splashed by rain, my complexion becomes damaged. A stage actor enjoys for himself the benefit that the audience is kept at such a far distance, that one cannot perceive if the fair hero's face is all paint and powder. I, however, must interact face to face, and sometimes it is more apparent than I should wish that my skin bears upon it an artificial crust of color.

It has always been somewhat more commonplace for women to wear this sort of cosmetic, than for men to employ it; but that is only because beauty is more of a necessity to the female sex, who have little else to use towards the enhancement of their positions or their gaining of friends. Men certainly *have* used it, for the last century or two, if not for longer. When I was a young man, it was still quite commonplace for the beaux and fops to paint their faces with washes and powders and rouge, sometimes even with the application of blacking to their eyebrows, or from time to time with a mouche on the face (though the mouche was more of a fashion in my grandfather's day, than it was by my time.) Therefore I thought nothing amiss in my own utilization of cosmetics. It is true it could be, at times, *unbecoming* if the coating were let to run or smear, or were applied with too heavy a hand; but the blotched and ruddy complexion given to me by nature, which this artifice concealed, was not any better to look upon, and therefore I deemed the *paint* to be the finer option.

It was not unusual that, when I should go to watch Brummell bathe in all his fascinating attention to detail, I would sometimes remain a while longer at his home after he had completed his task. His morning *toilette* often was not finished until well past a decent hour for breakfast, and so I might remain with him to dine or to drink, or to do both or all, well into the dark hours. On one particular day, during the warm season, I discovered myself in a sweat. Brummell took note of the impact which this had upon my face-paint.

"Why, Prinny, I think you have some thing on your face," said he.

I presumed he meant I had acquired a smear of soot or the like. I took up my handkerchief and went to the nearest mirror (his home was filled with them) but I could not find any thing of the sort. "Where is it?" I asked.

"All over," he replied.

I understood then that he meant my cosmetic. "Very funny, Mr. Brummell," said I, tho' not really finding it humorous at all. Still, I could perceive that my paint was not in its finest condition, and I began an effort to pat and blot it back into place over areas where it had faded and dripped away.

"Why must you wear that horrible muck?" he asked. "You know that those preparations destroy the complexion, rather than enhancing it."

"Mine is crafted by an excellent apothecary, who has omitted every harmful ingredient," said I, arguing with him. "It is very safe and I assure you it does much to enhance my appearance."

"Your Royal Highness does not need paint," said he, a tone of encouragement in his voice. "I am sure that with but a meager effort towards cleanliness and care of your health, you could have the most lovely complexion, without any thick powders or runny rouges."

"What advantage is it to wash one's face for an hour, rather than spend a quarter of one applying powder?"

He arched his eyebrow. "One's own face will not come off, in heat nor rain," was his reply.

That was a sound argument. "Yet, my misfortune is a deep-rooted redness of the face."

"From excess blood and a hot humor," said he, "exacerbated by that filth you rub all over your skin. Why not remedy the problem?"

"Oh, I have been down that course before," said I. "Years ago, I spoke to my physician about the matter. He agreed that heat and blood were what corrupted my complexion. He prescribed me to undertake daily leech treatments about my neck, and that I rub my skin with Galen's *Ceratum Refrigerans* to cool the heat. I followed this regimen devoutly, even tho' the Cerate seemed to actually aggravate my skin into eruptions. The physician assured me that it was merely my skin ridding itself of the built-up heat within, and that it would calm itself soon enough. I did think my color was improved by the leeches, at any rate. I continued to undergo the treatment, yet the effect which it produc'd, was always so maddeningly temporary! Within hours of it, my face would be flushed with color once again. I complained to the physician, who then suggested that instead of the Cerate, I should try to soak my face for a quarter-hour daily, in cold water chilled with ice that is brought in from up north, for this was a stronger coldness than the residual cold of the Cerate mixture. I therefore took to nearly drowning myself in a basin of such iced water every morning, to only come up for air as absolutely needed, even as the chilled liquid burnt and pained my flesh. Notwithstanding this, my skin became more smooth, and I think it did improve my appearance somewhat. From the shortness of breath this necessitated, I had to grow accustom'd to feelings of dizziness in the morning, but my face became fairer and cleaner than ever. I thought it was a mighty improvement, really."

"So why do you not continue?" asked Brummell.

I was aghast at that remark. Irritated, I answered him, "I *do*! I never put an *end* to this daily torture! Why, does my skin not look it?"

The Beau had the decency to keep quiet about the matter thereafter. Yet I was dismayed at this. His disapprobation of my *toilette* was quite evident, and somehow under Brummell's power it was coming to be seen as effeminate to use paint, just as it was to be caught wearing lace cuffs or pink floral embroideries. All of this had been very commonplace male dress at the time of

Brummell's birth: what change was he creating, what influence was it about him, that so redefined that which was considered *masculine?* It vexed me, that he possessed such power; but at this time I endured it, for even I was well under the spell of this most charming man and his impossibly handsome clothes.

Each day at five o'clock, men and women would ride out in their carriages at Hyde Park, attended by powdered footmen, to shew themselves and to see what was being shewn. Prior to five, however, the park was but a park. One was able to walk or ride there at pleasure. I sometimes took my phaeton for rides in that place, for I had two of the finest horses in England to pull me. If nobody was near, that might be endangered, I sometimes rode about as fast as I was able, just for the fun of it. It was such a delight! I loved the excitement of it, the sound of the wind around me and the blur which became of my surroundings. Horses and racing had been for ever counted amongst my most cherished delights. It was my favourite sport, well above any other.

One afternoon I was driving myself about the park in my most happy manner, whereupon I suddenly recognized that Brummell was at my side, speeding along in his curricle. Curricles are second-best to phaetons: a little heavier, but still quite lightweight, and powered by two horses. We greeted one another cheerfully, without halting our gallop.

"Good evening, Mr. Brummell," said I, calling above the roar of the wind.

"Good evening, your Highness," he answered. "Are you having a pleasant ride?"

"Splendid," I answered.

"Will you be staying for the promenade?"

"Perhaps. What time is it now?"

"About half past."

I had no idea of the hour. "Half past what?"

"Four."

"Oh! Is that why you are here? You are early."

"Yes, I went to see my glover this afternoon, but I had expected to pay him a lengthier visit. Can you believe it? The man provided me with nothing at all to complain about. He made an absolutely perfect pair of gloves. I do not need the thumbs made elsewhere, or any of the usual troubles. These London clothiers are genuinely beginning to know my needs!"

I remarked my astonishment, and then inquired of him whether he meant to pass the remainder of the time in the park.

"I think it sounds amusing enough," said he. "Would you care to race me?" he asked.

"I think we are already about it," I answered.

We continued our merry contention for speed and for obtaining the foremost spot. Sometimes he won. Sometimes I won. We were not placing wagers upon it, and so we barely kept any tally. We raced one another only for the fun of it: two gentlemen of fashion, looking to outdo one another howsoever we might.

After enough time had passed, we went together to Rotten Row, where the daily promenade took place. The *creme de la creme* were out in all their finery; but there was never to be found another man dressed better than I, or Mr. Brummell. He was already making a name for himself about London, darting through the city from dinner to ball to clubhouse in his tight breeches with daring French-style falls, his tastefully tasseled watch-cord dripping from his front pocket. His preference for muted colors was a great contrast to the floral tones we had admired in the previous century: he preferred blacks, browns and grays with only occasional bold hues of blue or burgundy to dress it up. This personal preference was spreading through the fashion like some sort of gangrene; every body was growing afraid of color, and even the gayest events began to look rather like funerals. Soon Almack's, the most fashionable ballroom in the entire country, had forbidden its gentlemen patrons from wearing any hue but black to their famous dances.

My own proclivities in fashion tended more towards spectacle than Brummell's: once he told me, "One wants to be seen, but not to attract attention. B----y Harlequin attracts attention, but a gentleman is merely regarded, without becoming a distraction." That is good enough advice for a common man, I suppose; but it was my duty to be seen. Thus I tended to dress with a little more flair and flash than Mr. Brummell would think appropriate. I enjoyed my brocades, embroideries and bright colors. I would improve my appearance with a smear of rouge or a dusting of white powder, rather than rely upon his *hygiene*. He made a push for simplicity, but by Heaven, just as with his morning baths, the amount of effort that was required for his version of simplicity, was too much for a man of the world, who had duties to attend!

On the whole, the Corinthians sided with me on this point. It was as ludicrous to simplify in Brummell's way, as it was for me to slim my figure with starvation rather than to avail myself to a tightening-belt.

Along with a few other Corinthians, we had created a little *cenacle*, at which we might from time to time meet to decide upon the hair or clothing styles which were to be display'd by us to the *bon ton*, or mull over the latest innovations to my regiment's military uniforms. Upon one certain afternoon, we engrossed ourselves in the examination of some sketches of the uniforms. Some particular regiment or another had an ensemble which I believed could be improved upon. I conceived some desire to add more ribbands to the sleeves. Brummell, on the other hand, agreed that these sleeves could be improved upon, but in his mind it was to be done by stripping away the accessories, rather than by adding to them. He was always in love with simplicity. We quarrelled a little about it: really it was a mere nothing, or so I thought at the time. Our companions weighed in, agreeing with one or the other of us as they wished. In time it grew dark out; Brummell was forc'd to excuse himself for some appointment to be kept that evening. The matter of the uniforms was yet undecided, when he bade his good byes, but before he parted, Brummell winked to his friends and advised them: "Help Prinny to see the light."

He left, and I was a little annoyed at the manner in which he had done so. "The decision is mine, not his," I declared, "and I will not be moved just because George Brummell has the idea."

"That is a given," said Lord Beaufort, who was one of our secret circle. "And you know that we will ultimately side with you, because you are always right about these matters." It always gladdened my heart to hear compliments of that sort.

"Aye," asserted another, "that young buck has a good eye for day-to-day dress, but not as much good sense as your Royal Highness when it comes to ceremony. Really, Brummell would be nothing without your guidance."

I was soothed by these words, bestowed by my loyal sycophants; and with the troubled waters of my temper oiled down, I was feeling more capable to make my choices. I resolved to have the sleeves bedecked with one added row of ribband, which much pleased the members of the circle.

Some time later, when Brummell learnt of the decision, he reproached me with the words: "Looking to make maypoles of your soldier's limbs, are you?"

CHAPTER 4.

The Bawd to Lust's Abuse

In leone cataphagae nascuntur et imperiosi, it is said. Perhaps I do live up to my natal chart, if that is the case. It is, at least, some thing to which I can aspire.

As Prince, my birth-day on August the twelfth has always been treated as a national holiday. People put on private dinners in my honor, and the military makes shews and parades. On this one particular year, I had decided to put on a great celebration in honor of the event, at my London home of Carlton House. Afterall, if I cannot take joy in my own birth, how can I expect as much from any body else?

The marks of a truly great party are threefold: the first is that all society in attendance must have a perfectly enjoyable time. The second is that every body should leave with a story to tell, and preferably that they will tell and retell for years to come. The third is that there must be some form of spectacle, to be entertained by.

I had a new suit of clothes to wear on that day. My coat was a fine blue silk, with a black jacquard collar. My waistcoat was vertical stripes of black and brown. I added a yellow sash to embellish it all. I looked very well; even stunning: but unfortunately, either I had put on a little additional weight since the time of the fitting, or as I think more likely, the tailor had mistaken his measurements. I did not quite fit into my waistcoat, and there was no time to make revisions to the garment; however, the trouble was easily resolved by adjusting my tightening-belt so that it was laced a bit more snugly about me than normal. Alas! That extra restriction was enough to keep me in agony throughout the evening! I must own that despite the gaiety of the event, and my fondness for my company, I found myself to be in not the best of spirits. How could one be, when one's innards are squeez'd to the point that they should burst, taught laces cut into the flesh of one's back, and all one's flow of blood is dammed up at the waist? To the restricted sensation, one grows acclimated, by the frequent wearing of such a garment; yet a sudden additional tightening of it by even a small degree can produce the utmost pain and physical torment.

Thus I sat, quiet and sullen at what ought to have been a most marvellous dinner. I could take some pride that at least my guests seem'd to enjoy themselves, while my body ached. My closest friends, and most of my family, were in attendance: even Caroline was there, albeit only because my Royal mother had insisted that I should invite her, in order to keep up appearances. I made a point not to talk to her. I began to drink heavily of the available brandy, largely in the hope that it might have the capacity to dull my physical discomfort. I forced myself to eat a little of the food, but found scarcely any delight in it. It was my good fortune that Brummell was there, his pristine linens shimmering in the candle-light as he kept the table enlivened with those exercises of non-wit that have come to be known as *Brummelliana*: statements so vacant in their content that they seem nearly as if they were wise, and which always made for much laughter.

"Do you never eat vegetables, Mr. Brummell?" asked Frederica upon noting his plate was heavy with meats, and the few vegetal specimens that had found their way on, were untouched.

"Of course I do, madam. I think that I once ate a pea," he replied. Then, to further elaborate upon his distaste for vegetables, he told a story of a friendship which he had put to an end: "I had great reluctance in cutting the connexion, but what could I do? I discovered that the wretch positively ate *cabbage*."

48

When the tablecloths were removed and the sweets and cheese were brought, Brummell railed against those who would sate themselves upon cheese accompanied by beer. "A gentleman never malts with his cheese, he always ports."

When the dinner was finished, there was dancing; yet by this time I was so unwell that I was obliged to excuse myself. Why, I should have fainted straight away had I been foolish enough to attempt any thing so vigorous as to dance, when I was already drenched in sweat and gasping for air. I was eager to be freed, at least briefly, from the torturous confines of my corset. I stole myself away to a little broom-closet just off of the Corinthian Room, in which I thought I could find adequate solitude to undo my waistcoat and let out the strings of my tightening-belt, for at least a few minutes, that I could recover my senses and rejoin with the festivities which were mainly confined to the Conservatory, by this time. When the strings were loos'd, I felt instantly at ease, and even a bit hungry. I regretted that I had been able to partake only of the most meager mouthfuls of the sumptuous meal that had been served up so soon before.

As I stood alone in that dark room, delighting in my moment of solace, I soon found much to my consternation that I was still to be in some company. The door was opened: I was instantly dismayed, for I was surely in no condition to interact with any sort of society. Rather than be put into an awkward position with this visitor, I stepped back to conceal myself behind a cabinet. In the dark of the room, I was out of sight, being able to neither see or to be seen by the importune company. I could tell only at first that they were male and female, and as I listened to their conversation, I came to recognize that the gentleman was none other than George Brummell. The woman's voice was more difficult to place, but it was familiar to me. Her speech was accented towards the teutonic, altho' amongst my friends and family that was nothing peculiar, for many of my cousins were German, and several other Hanoverian nobles resided in the city. It was quite certain, in any event, that this couple before me believed themselves to be in a situation of total privacy, or else they should not have gone forward with so exceedingly intimate a conversation as that which commenced:

"Nobody shall see us in here," said Brummell. He did not often become intoxicated, but neither was he immune to the powers of alcoholic spirits. His tone implied that this was an evening whereupon he had somewhat overindulged.

"I can scarcely see *you*," the woman answered him, "and I think you must scarcely see me. You are not ashamed of me, are you, that I am a bit old?"

"Aw, there is nothing to be ashamed for," said he. "Why, the Prince has a genuine Catholic relic for a mistress, and he flaunts her proudly enough. But notwithstanding that, I figure that a lady who is a little wiser can put that maturity of mind to good use."

It may appear indecent or lewd of me to have eavesdropped upon all of this, unintended tho' it was; but the fact is, that I was more afraid for what disfavour Brummell and his friend should think of *me*, were I discovered half dressed in a closet, than I was discomfited by the knowledge of their activity. I could next detect what sounded like kissing, possibly followed by a hurried ------. I certainly made no attempt to look upon my friend or to interrupt him, though I did feel rather irked by his maligning of Maria to this utter stranger. In time, their talk resum'd:

"We really must find more comfortable means to meet one another," said he. "This is positively shameful: I would sooner wear a floral-pattern coat."

"I know," said the woman, "but my husband is always about, and it seems as if eyes are for ever upon me."

"Well, they are certainly always upon *me*. If you wish for privacy, you shall have to find yourself another beau."

"This Beau suits me well enough," she answered in an affectionate tone, "but let us be gone, before our absence becomes known."

The two of them left, with those words. I remained behind the cabinet for some minutes longer, coursing with a mixture of agitation and befuddlement for what I had just overheard. I was left to wonder at his mystery woman. I would not call Beau Brummell a stranger to the ladies; but he was not known to love them. He was pleased enough to grant them his society, but always more likely to gratify himself with a well trained prostitute than to pursue any earnest courtship, at least in all the time that I had known him. Who was the mysterious creature that had caught his hard-to-please fancy? Evidently she was older, and married. I suppose I could understand why one might find that to be desirable, for my own tastes in women often followed a like variety.

I fastened my tightening-belt, waistcoat and sash by myself, and return'd to the festivities. For the remainder of the night, I kept my eye upon Brummell, hoping to catch him give a glance or an intimate caress to some female in attendance and thus betray to me the object of his affection, but he kept his secret well concealed. In the meanwhile, merry-making went on: the *haute ton* of my guests kept about their dancing, gaming and gossip until the dawn broke thro' the sky.

At last, when party was broken up and the final guests were gone, I retir'd to my own room and cast away the uncomfortable garments in which I had passed my whole night. Freed at long last, I was enabl'd to eat once again. I called for my favourite breakfast to be brought to me: three beefsteaks and two pigeons, washed down with the most delicious white wine, port and brandy. It was a good beginning to my first day of a new year of life.

I was still curious, in regards to the mystery of Brummell's paramour; and over the ensuing days, the brashness to inquire with him directly about her identity was, little by little, built up within me. I wondered whether I ought to tell him how I had overheard him: good heavens, he was with her in a house that was not his own, so certainly he must have known that lack of privacy was a risque which he bore? Ah, but I too have been so moved by passions, as to throw out all caution and abandon myself to my feelings. I decided not to shame him, and to ask him only amicably for information regarding his affairs.

My opportunity was presented, when I went to amuse myself at one of his morning levées. One or two other gentlemen were also there to watch him bathe, but I alone remained into tea time. We took a little of the hot beverage, but mainly we sated ourselves with good sherry, that afternoon. As we debated whether or not to afterward go on promenade in St. James or Hyde park, the particular benefit of Hyde was mentioned: that benefit being that *ladies* were more likely to be there unchaperon'd.

"...And really," said Brummell, "I do not much like to promenade at St. James, because the ground is so dusty there, and the gravel cuts up one's shoes till they look more like sandals."

"Oh, really, Brummell," said I, "you only say that as an excuse to sit with the ladies."

He smiled at me. "Aw, we do not spend so much time dressing ourselves just to draw the eyes of men alone!" he answered.

"Clothes do cross the barriers of every thing, even of language," said I, spotting in here my chance and going in for the kill. "Why, I hear tales that you have formed an attachment to a German lady."

Brummell appeared discomfited by that, though he fast endeavor'd to compensate with his customary smiles and jokes. "Why, who says such things? They must not have a good imagination. Surely, a Chinese or an African lady would have made for a better scandal."

"Is it, then, untrue?" I asked in feigned innocence.

He took out his snuff box that he might make a pretext for the delaying of his answer. The box was gilded, with a scene of Jason and Medea painted across the top. When he was ready to speak, he replied, "Aw, Prinny, you know how it is. It's not gentlemanly to advertise one's intimate affairs with respectable women. It may be true that I know a German or a Fleming or a Swede, but I could not tell any more than that, with dignity. I am not a Prince: it would be a degradation for me to report on my affinities."

"I then presume that it is some shameful relationship?"

"Maybe it would be best were you to tell me what it was you were told," said he. "I can answer you better, if I know what I am charg'd with."

Now I took out my snuff box, of blue and black enamel, with gold frames and set with pearls, the head of Minerva upon it. It proffer'd to me an added moment to collect my thoughts. "You were reported to have been in the presence of a German woman, at my birth-day celebration. That is all I have on it."

Brummell was fighting not to betray his feelings through his face. "Well, half the people at your birth-day were German, so that ought to have surpriz'd nobody. Some people might call *you* a German."

"You are not embroiling yourself with members of my own family, are you?" I asked with raised eyebrows. Brummell laughed nervously at that, whereupon I realized that the woman probably *was* some relation of mine: and that being the case, it was unlikely that I should meet with success in any effort to provoke him to reveal her identity to me, as he might fear I could take it for an insult. In hindsight, I conceive that I *ought* to have been insulted; but at the time my interest was only towards the gaining of information. Thus, I laughed it all off, and I made a little joke that we should promenade at the docks, if we were to find foreign ladies that would be to his taste.

Ultimately our promenade was made at Green Park. It was our last promenade of the season, before we packed up to visit our friends in their country homes, for the autumn. It was usual that every body in the *ton* left London when the season was over, and moved instead to country estates or to fashionable cities such as Bath or Brighton or Scarborough. Brummell was a well-loved character, and so notwithstanding that he did not hold any country seats of his own, he rarely wanted an invitation to another's. We would not see each other again till the following year, although we certainly kept in communication.

CHAPTER 5.

Sick-Thoughted Venus

The populace seem to be possessed of a profound wish to know just whom shall next sit as their ruler, even if the transition may yet be decades away. My own family took claim of the throne despite that they were German and not English, in consequence of the previous incumbents having died without issue. Their cousins in Hanover were called upon, by necessity, to fill the gap: my great-grandfather George was the first of them, followed by my grandfather George who outlived his expected heir, thus leaving the duty to be taken by my father, the third George. It is presumed that I shall one day become the fourth George. Should it pass that I leave no heirs behind me, it is to be expected that to choose the next in succession will become a horrifying jumble for every body. There could very well be a debacle like that of the sixteenth century, wherein Henry VIII's son died at the age of fifteen, unmarried, leaving his cousin Lady Jane Gray to rule as Queen for all of nine days before her unpopularity saw her to the chopping block; after which "Bloody" Mary was installed as ruler and passed the next five years advancing the death of any body who did not adhere to her ideas concerning religion. When she died childless, it was her sister Elizabeth that came to power, and though she ruled long, she too died childless, and from this misfortune of the country being left to choose a new monarch came several decades of religious wars.

Already in my life we had seen, in France, what horrors might happen if the Royal family were cast out; and an English Buonaparte was the last thing that any body wanted. It was therefore considered a vital duty, upon me, for a sure heir to be made to exist.

While my Royal father's personal motives may have been merely to ruin me, this need for heirs was ultimately the reason why Parliament had wish'd to force me to marry Caroline. No children I might have with Maria would be viewed as legitimate, and yet I had no desire for children with any body else. When my apeish cousin Caroline came to me direct from the Principality of Brunswick-Wolfenbüttel, the hope behind the arrangement of this marriage, was for the two of us to produce an heir to the English throne. It had taken all my willpower to be able to perform on our wedding night, but nine months to the day from that disastrous ceremony, she gave birth to our daughter Charlotte. Thus I need not bother myself anymore with that dull-witted Caroline, who at this time kept quite to herself in Blackheath: or in any event, kept herself away from me. Sheer luck had seen Charlotte born to us, but she is female, which can render succession a tricky business: depending upon whom she marries, she might not even find herself eligible to serve as Queen. Why, even *I* should have been excluded from the line of succession, would any body of consequence regard my marriage to Maria as being legal.

For this reason I held immense hope that my brother, Frederick, would see things through with his wife, Frederica, in producing a spare to the heir. Frederica is a charming woman, of suitable German Royal lineage, with crude looks and spotless repute. She would be an ideal mother to any future monarch. Additionally, the pressure upon me to reunite or reconcile with that gorgon Caroline would be subdued at so long last, would only a male heir be brought forth by their branch. Truly it would be a great relief to me, and every one, would it but happen. My hopes were great that it should be so. Yet my hopes were to be most sourly disappointed: the best-dress'd, most well-scrubb'd figure in England was about to make a shambles of them.

Lord and Lady Jersey were friends to me, both before and after my romantic entanglement with the latter of them. George, Lord Jersey, understood the situation. It was not unheard of in society at that time, for male friends to sometimes find themselves *en amours* with the same woman, even if one man might chance to be her husband. Marriages were so often contracted for reasons other than those lofty ideals of love, that it was difficult for us to begrudge a spouse who had found that oft-desired emotion elsewhere. George and I did not hold any jealousies against one another, and I sometimes even included him amongst my group of Corinthians. His wife Frances, however, was always a bit conniving. You may recall that it was she that had chosen Caroline for my wife, a feat for which I never forgave her. I had called off our romance; yet, we remained on affable terms; pleasant and affable enough that I was invited to a ball at their house one evening, during the season. The companion I wanted to have on my arm, was my one and only Maria: I had done every thing in my power to maintain a friendship with her, and to seek to restore her favourable opinion of me after I had been oblig'd to marry Caroline. I had even written out my Will and Testament, naming her as my one true wife, and leaving only a shilling to that stinking Brunswickan *Weibsstück*. My efforts were bearing fruit: Maria had agreed to attend this party with me, as my companion. Our relationship was understood by every one: I had never tried to hide my darling Maria from my friends. I am too pleased with her, to harbour any design to conceal her from others, for she is a sparkling creature, and even as she ages she keeps her dignity and feminine force about her. Her presence fills a room like none other. I am, meanwhile, her young lover, her handsome little Prince who is devoted to her; and all the world may know me in this role.

The events of that night were gay, and resplendent with *ton*. All the finest of London were at the ball. The ladies were dressed in their slightly sheer Grecian gowns, the skirts of which had recently been narrowed by the Gods of the Mode, in order to better expose and exhibit their shapes. The men were in the black or blue evening coats, chins held high by braces concealed beneath their tall white collars and cravats. Hair-powder was rarely worn anymore, except by the older gentlemen; however, in my case my hair was endeavoring to color *itself* a hue of mostly white, and I sometimes combed a bit of powder through to even out the tone of it. It matched with my face powder to make an alliance of color that was actually rather becoming, I thought. It remained my preference to dress myself in bright hues; and especially for so happy an event as a ball, I could not bear to clothe myself in only somber blacks and browns. On that night I wore yellow breeches and a blue jacket: my favourite color combination.

Dancing took place in one room, cards in another, *per usitate*. No event of the *ton* was ever complete without Mr. Brummell's attendance, and naturally he was there, his smooth-scrubbed skin gleaming in the candlelight, holding a paper set of hearts and spades in his hand. The man was able to dance, but at a ball, it was always in the card room that one would find him, or else standing back to criticize the dancers who performed feats he dared not to attempt by himself. He was now in his middle twenties, and already the inheritance which had become his own upon his twenty-first birth-day, was dwindling. On clothes alone he spent over £1,000 a year; and he spent freely on all the other luxuries required for the life of a London beau. I am under the impression that he did have a small amount invested in the funds, but for the most part he relied upon the card table for his upkeep. The *ton* absolutely adored this pass-time: it seemed that the illegality of the act only magnified their enjoyment of it. To game for money was not, strictly speaking, legal; but it was nevertheless very commonplace. As long as it was done in private, as at a home or in a club, its criminality was overlooked: certainly nobody shrunk from doing it within Prinny's eyesight, and I enjoyed it often enough myself. High wagers were entirely usual. I have heard of as much as £40,000 to be lost in a single game. With stakes so high, a man like Brummell stood to gain, or to lose, vastly.

I observed, this night, that Brummell was at a game of *vingt-et-un*. His friend, the buck Pierrepoint, was one of those who played against him. As I approached, the pair were at a draw, each scoring some equal number in their cards: I forget now what it was, let us say fifteen. They were each dealt another card. Pierrepoint turned up his, and found it a five of clubs. At Brummell's turn, he flipped his card to shew a ten of spades, *alias* lost. Naturally his face betrayed some signs of dismay, but he was seasoned to the frown of Fortune, and had hopes that he might cheer her before the night was over. He passed to his friend a few banknotes: these were used for high-stakes games of this nature, where the weight of many coins would be too cumbersome to carry all night long. Soon a second round was begun. Cards were dealt to the players. Brummell flipped his couple: two aces were his bounty. He look'd at the hand of his rival, and already knew no hope to win.

"Well," said he at his discovery, "someone bring me a pistol, so I may shoot myself." Every one laughed at his quip. He emptied his pockets to pay out the debt (gambling debts were always paid at once, or else assured with a I.O.U., for these were debts of honor.) After he had fulfilled this duty, he set about his new endeavors to recoup what he had lost.

Meanwhile, Maria and I enjoyed ourselves in a lovely time. We danced to the musick, and per my duties as a gentleman, I did ask some of the other available women to dance, as well; but I cannot dance too long, or my sides begin to ache, and I grow very short of breath. I am not alone in this, and that is precisely why there are card rooms. I would vanish there to catch my breath or to play a quick game, between bouts. From time to time I would look upon Brummell's progress. I could see that the night was not treating him kindly, for time and again I observed him to pass a banknote to someone across the table. Notwithstanding this, he was always looking to bear it cheerfully, that he would not spoil the evening by allowing himself to become dismayed.

At length I was distracted from this display by the call of Maria's voice: "George," she said, meaning me but provoking half the men in the room to look up, "it is past one. You promised not to keep me up all night long."

I understood that she was conveying to me her wish to depart. As the two of us kept separate houses and we had arrived separately, we did not have to leave together; but as I was her escort for the evening, it was expected that I should at least see her safely to her carriage. I went to her side and began to search out our hosts amongst the revellers, so that she could bid them a good night.

While it happened that we roamed the rooms, on the hunt for Lord and Lady Jersey, it came to my attention that Brummell was behind us, and tracing our steps. Evidently he too had plans to leave.

"Spent out, Brummell?" I inquired.

"Aw, I did not lose more than I could afford to, but I have some other commitments to-night," he said in answer.

"Do not tell me you have another ball to attend!"

"Aw, no. Nothing of the kind." I could see him color a shade upon his unpainted cheeks as he spoke, as if he were either abash'd, or lovestruck, or both.

This intrigued me. "Some lady you cannot go to see in broad daylight?" I asked.

Maria interrupted us. "George, do not teaze him," she said to me. "You know how he bites. Let us find Frances, so I can go to bed."

The three of us wove about the house in hunt of our hosts, in the course of which time my mind began its own meanderings, to the subject of Brummell's assignation. My curiosity had been utterly piqued. I knew Brummell to be the most fastidious, fussy and critical creature I had ever befriended. He had never openly displayed any thing in the way of *tendresse* towards women: why, had I not overheard him with the German woman at Carlton House *per accidens*, I might have wondered whether he was attracted to women at all, or else if he was, like Adonis, too busy and thoroughly satisfied with himself to be at all tempted by the attractions offered of Venus. What creature could have stirred the passions of the perpetually cool beau? What creature of such beauty and fashion might have moved him to love? Was it the same woman from Carlton House last year? My mind heated and raced. I felt as if I had had *had* to learn the secret, for my own gratification, nay, consolation, for the questions and fantastications as to what sort of beauty it could be would surely gall my mind unceasingly. Therefore, very hastily, I devised a very simple plan for discovering my answer: I would follow him in secret, and learn where it was that he should go.

In good time we were able to locate Frances, to bid good night to her. I turn'd to speak to Brummell.

"Sir, I am not intending to leave this party just yet. Would you do me the honor of seeing Mrs. Fitzherbert to her carriage?"

Maria displayed signs that she was somewhat vexed by the way that I was foisting her off to Mr. Brummell, but I sweetly explained to her how the arrangement made much better sense, than for me to excuse myself to see her out, only to come back in again. "Besides, Brummell is the most fashionable man in town, save myself. It is an honor to be seen out by him."

She gave her consent to the arrangement, as did Brummell. He offered his arm to her, and she took it.

Together the two of them approached Frances, to excuse themselves to her.

Meanwhile, I hurried myself to the door of the house unaccompanied. I did not tell any body of my intention to leave, but I smuggled myself out the door unobserved. I had come to this gathering in my phaeton, which I now took up again, and fast as I could I drove the vehicle out of sight of the house. I was scarcely hid in the shadows before I saw Brummell and Maria appear at the steps, arm in arm; once outside, the handsome Beau called, much too loudly, for "*Mistress* Fitzherbert's carriage."

I groaned. I could overlook his rudeness as being perhaps an honest mistake of pronunciation: we did sometimes say *mistress* in that context, thirty years prior, before he was even born. Perhaps he was but being fastidious in vocalizing the normally silent T and R. Still, Maria never let me hear an end to it, complaining of the slight for years to come. She suspects his announcing of her as a *mistress* was a deliberate insult, attributing his conduct to an ill-considered effort to ingratiate himself with the hostess, by degrading her one-time rival. Notwithstanding the abuse, Maria took the coach, and Brummell soon took his own in suit.

I followed the Beau's curricle across the near-empty streets of the city, keeping far enough behind to, I hoped, evade his detection. My heart pounded with worry, but I imagined that, would he have seen me, I could always make the pretense to have simply left the party immediately after him. In any event, to spin such a yarn was unneeded: for I cannot presume he would have continued as he did, would he have recognized me in pursuit of him.

We traveled in the direction of St. James. I felt very naughty for what I did, but proud that I had discovered this ruse to achieve my aim. I deeply wish'd to see a glimpse of Brummell's mystery maiden — or matron, perhaps, if he was able to visit her alone at night. What might she be? Surely a great beauty, I thought. Perhaps she was some young widow, or a neglected wife of some English lord. She must have a face like an angel, whatever she was; I could not think that Brummell would have settled for any thing less than perfection personified.

At length he came to a stop. I hasten'd to turn off and observe his movements from a distance. He alighted from his coach directly in front of a house that I knew too well. It was York House: my brother Frederick's property. At first I wondered if he meant to proceed on foot to some adjacent building, but I saw him waved in by the sentinel as if expected, and then to proceed to the very door of the home where my own family members dwelt. At first I was perplexed. My brother was away. What person at York House could he mean to visit?

Then, in all horror, it struck me.

He was there for Frederica.

She was the German girl from the Corinthian Room.

Frederica: the decent, noble cousin, in whose hands I had rested all too many hopes for the perpetuation of our Royal family!

She is not even all that attractive. Of all people, *she* had captured Brummell's fancy?

It could not be so. There had to be some other explanation. I suppose I could have followed them inside, if I had wish'd, for the guards would recognize me and surely would not turn me away; but I would likely only send Brummell running out through some back entry to make his escape, and perhaps provide Frederica with the opportunity to invent some innocent explanation for her conduct. I took up my spyglass from my pocket (all the men of fashion carried one) and with it I endeavor'd to gain some better insight as to what was taking place within the house; but whatever it was that Brummell and Frederica were about, they had sense enough not to go about it in front of an unshuttered window. I could see nothing. I was left only to imagine what went on behind those walls.

Brummell, Brummell, how could you do this to your friend Prinny? Was it Frederica's bankroll that drew you into her arms? It could not be her beauty, for certain. And Frederica: why? Have you no sense of your duties?

How could the two of you conspire to break the heart of your friend in this way, and dash the hopeful dreams he had for the future? Can you not conceive of what injury this selfish action of yours has made upon him, and to his heartfelt wishes to reconcile with Maria? Why, if Frederica cannot be entrusted to produce the next in line for the Royal throne, the person who will have to see it through is your poor, unhappy, wretched, luckless George *Princeps*, who has a Princess he cannot abide.

I returned, so dismayed, to Jersey's ball; for my curiosity was now too well satiated. I was in infinitely poorer spirits than I had been when I departed. I stayed on and partook of my friends' brandy, awaking the next morning on their drawing room floor, where I had gone drunkenly asleep and been permitted to remain undisturbed. A sheet was draped over me for comfort. I was wished good morning by my hosts, who were both familiar with my tendencies to overdrink at these events; they avoided any direct mention of my condition on the prior night; and after my assuring them that I was well, I drove myself home, to Carlton House, where I went to bed, full of regrets for my discovery. I considered whether I should confront the Beau, but would that really stop him? In all likelihood it would serve only to humiliate myself and my family, and risque the general exposure of such an interloper. Brummell was too haughty to even take my advice about the material of his waistcoat, never mind what I thought of his choice in mistresses; and this was hardly a case of thinking her beneath him, indeed the trouble was that she was too fine for the likes of him. Yet I had to resign myself to it: Brummell was Frederica's lover, and she was his.

***

"You asked me to that ball as your companion, yet you could not remain by me for even a whole evening. This fickleness of yours, George, is so wholly unattractive a trait that it overshadows every good quality which you can claim."

Maria had not taken it kindly that I had foisted her off onto Brummell at the end of Lord Jersey's ball. She disliked Brummell in general: for though she agreed that he was a fine figure to look upon, she did not approve of the criticisms and abuses which he utilized in lieu of wit. His final public insult against her was too great an affront for her to bear, especially when the story of it began to circulate about the town. I admit, I was upset by it as well; though my rage may have been enhanced by my newfound knowledge of the Beau's impropriety with my sister-in-law. I told Maria that I would cut Brummell from my society, but this was altogether insufficient to give her any

71

satisfaction. She was very annoyed that I had not seen her home myself, and that I had not been with her to defend her from Brummell's affront, and that her degradation had become a scandal.

"I am sorry," said she, "but this being the circumstance, I cannot continue to see you, or be a part of your world."

It was rare that Maria and I ever truly quarrelled. She was always very agreeable, even when she disagreed with me. Over the course of twenty years' marriage, she had developed a stratagem for how to handle me, when she had endured altogether too much of me and found my behavior turned intolerable. It was: to simply call an end to our relationship, and flee from me. She preferr'd to break my heart rather than to risque my wrath. For my own part, out of pride I withheld my tears and made every affectation of solemn agreement to all her horrible terms, but at the very moment I was returned home, I fell into a swoon.

From there, my unrelenting agony compelled that I wept and howled for days. My heart and mind were devastated by her loss. I was confined to my bed, my whole body wasting and dying of sorrow. I was oh! so feverish and short of breath: I was certain that I would expire at any moment, and my waking each morning came to me as a disappointing surprize. Soon, word of my condition became known about the city. I hoped that Maria would hear of it, and regret her actions, and that she would come back to me; but this did not occur.

On the third day of my illness, none other than Beau George Brummell came to me, to pay his good wishes to his dying friend. As you might imagine, I was none too pleased with him at that time, but obviously I could not very well say that I was not at home. He was shewn into the chamber. He bore a wrapped object under his arm, and when he saw me, and the woeful state to which I was reduced, his reaction was one of utter discomfiture.

"My God, Prinny," he cried, true sympathy in his tone. "What has that monstrous woman done to you?"

My heart wanted to explode with my sadness. Brummell's willingness to provide a listening ear did much to mend my perturbation with him, very rapidly. "Oh, Brummell! It's awful: Maria says she will not see me anymore! My own wife!" I groaned and fainted backwards onto my pillow, upsetting the box of *bon bons* which I had left there.

Brummell hasten'd to my side. There was brandy on my nightstand: he poured some and waved the glass under my nose. The fumes revived me, but I remained on the verge of tears.

"I cannot go on, Brummell! Oh, I should have died when she first sought to leave me, when I was married off to that ugly German b---h: I could have been spared from all this wretchedness and misery!"

Brummell put the brandy glass into my hand. I drank it, striving not to sob as I did so. He then sat upon the bed with me, very casually and comfortably.

"I brought you a get-well gift," he said. He presented me with the wrapped object he had carried in, which in turn I opened with some interest. Viewing it through the blur of tears, I found that within the package was the most darling little snuff box known to man. I felt better immediately, merely from looking upon the wonderful *object d'art*. It was a box of elaborate enameled design, with a little miniature portrait of myself in military garb atop. It was based upon a full-sized painting that had been made of me some years before, which I had always felt to be one of my most flattering. The original was no longer in my possession, so I was pleased for Brummell's gift of a copy, in convenient snuff box form.

"That brought some color back to your face," said Brummell encouragingly. "Rouse up, Prinny. You only need to get out of this dreary bedchamber to feel better. Let us go out shopping! That shall cheer you up, I have no doubt on it."

The notion of shopping did appeal to me, but still, I did not agree to it. My soul was too wounded. "No, I am *dying*," I said wretchedly. "I have been destroyed by the abuses and heartless conduct of those whom I loved best and had the greatest reason to expect should treat me kindly. I shall never leave this bed again!"

"We can go to the club afterwards!" he urged still more brightly.

Now, that was sufficient to tempt me. A bit of fun did seem like it might have power to restore me to some approximation of health and wellness. I considered whether my constitution was fit to endure it, and soon determined that it might be possible. "You had better not be the death of me, Brummell," I said, throwing off the bedclothes. I rang for my valets, and after some while was pass'd to get me dressed, Brummell and I set out for an afternoon of acquisition. We took my carriage and brought some liveried servants to carry away our purchases. Bond Street was our destination that day: the place of hatters, gunsmiths, tailors, bootmakers, booksellers, perfumers and jewelers. It was where the men of fashion went to shop. Brummell and I have spent ourselves into debt there many times: most of the shopkeeps knew us by sight, and those who did not, could tell nevertheless by our exquisite dress and the number of servants that followed us, that we had money to burn: or at least that we had creditors backing our debts. Shawls, jewels, perfumes and hats were our bounty, in numbers that would supply a normal man for months; but us, we were likely to buy as much again in another week to come. Still, I found the event to be as revivifying as a trip to the spa. I felt much better, and in thanks, I backed Brummell's gaming at Brooks' club that night, which was the place we went to afterward. He won £100 straight off, having on the previous day wagered with another member that he would have me out of my sick-bed by that night.

CHAPTER 6.

Contenting But the Eye

Brummell did not have a great deal of money, in comparison to what he spent; and the little that he did earn was made, almost without exception, at the gaming tables. Yet, the consequence of my association with him assured that his debts always went uncollected for lengthy, even indefinite periods. With the moneylenders off his hip, Brummell was able to beg and borrow to his heart's content, and to surround himself with a manner of living that was the utter envy of the *beau monde*. Excursions to enjoy the pleasures of Brighton and the spa towns were commonplace, but London remained ever the center of his world. I remember the days when I would be alone, watching in fascination as he groomed himself; but after a few years of marking my example, it had come that dozens of people, men and women alike, attended daily to watch him. The street in front of his home was cluttered with coaches and horses; his hallways were overflowing with society, with jewelers and tailors, with artists, with pretty young girls and their chaperons, each and every one of them seeking an audience with the great Beau Brummell. His bachelor townhouse was not a large one, and it was woefully inadequate for the sheer quantity of his guests, but he was not in a financial position to take up any grander estate for the comfort of their reception; not if he wish'd to attend to his own comforts in the meantime.

For what did these people come to Brummell? Many simply wish'd to receive his attention in guise of his advice. As he grew older and more self assured, his compliments became more scarce; yet even to receive his insults seem'd to fill people with a certain delight. There is a story of a particular Duke who went to Brummell's house, evidently whilst harbouring a suspicion of some inferiority in the cut of his new clothes. He asked Brummell particularly what he thought of the coat. Brummell made a shew of scrutinizing the garment, at the end of which he cried, "Sir, do you even *call* this thing a coat?" The Duke was happy enough to tell and retell this little adventure as if it were a point of pride; and other like tales circulated all through the city, adding to the Beau's reputation for strict good taste, even at the expense of manners. It sounds like a paradox, does it not? Yet we all knew that manners were flexible: what one may do in Bath is not what one may do in London. Meanwhile, Beauty was a fixed idea, and one for which Brummell seem'd to have an exceptional view. So, we listened to him, as if he were some priest of Venus, proclaiming to us what sacrifices we should make at her altar if we were to receive her favours and be blessed with the love and loveliness over which she ruled. The insults he dish'd out were like part of a game, and his friends were not faulted if they threw back any like abuse in his direction — tho' there was rarely cause to try, for every thing he undertook was done with such impeccability that it would be but idiotick nonsense to even attempt to disparage his dress or his *toilette*. Still, the insults were accepted amongst us. It was simply a mark of our constant competition to be the best.

Notwithstanding all his impertinence, Brummell did make efforts to court and keep his powerful friends; even me. He hung my portrait at his home, along with other pictures of his worthy companions. He would make little gifts to us: tokens so that we would be continually assured that he thought of us and wished us all the best. But they were merely calculated little games, political actions with no substance. I knew them well, myself. And yet they were effective! How much, alas! does the human soul long for flattery, love and acceptance, that it will chase even the most insincere echoes of those moods? And why moreso when they are bestowed by a person whom one has come, for whatever reason, to admire?

Thus I kept him for my companion. God help me, I did *like* him. I adored him, even. I could see his flaws and yet they did not matter, somehow: at least, they did not seem to kill my sense of all his brilliance and charm. So, just as every one else, I went to him for advice, invited him to attend me, and basked in the flattery of his company. I sought to keep him as a friend, and under this cloak of friendship I overlooked and forgave his little missteps, imagining each time that he must have learnt his lesson and would not do it again.

He always rose late, and in London it was characteristick for a "morning" to run well into the afternoon. I went to visit him one day during the period that a metropolite might refer to as morning. I had at this time conferr'd to him several tasks involving the redecoration of some rooms at Carlton House, and I recognized that a few of the tradesmen involved with this procedure were waiting, in the halls, for an audience with him. Other noble faces, that I knew, were arranged against the walls, countenanced in a sort of dull worry and anxiety for their allotted time. When the valet shewed me in, he made an offer to interrupt Brummell's present meeting in order to announce me, but I was in no hurry that day; I knew that others had waited longer, some of whom I considered my friends; and as I passed the servant his tip, I replied that he should let the others have their turn. I imagined that I would pass the time by conversing with some of the others that waited, but nobody demonstrated themselves to be particularly chatty that day, or at least, I somehow held no appeal to them for more than a cursory greeting and polite nodding of the head to whatever I spoke. They were all anxious to see Brummell and Brummell alone. *What was a Prince compared to Brummell?*

I proceeded down the hall towards where the Beau held his meeting, thinking I might in that case occupy myself by eavesdropping upon whatever conversation was held at that time. I harboured some hopes that it might be some thing concerning the work at Carlton House which I had appointed him to oversee.

As I have said, his dwelling was not a large house; and much of his conversation could be easily deciphered by those waiting in the hallway, even through the barrier of the shut door. What I could hear within, certainly did pertain to me; but it was not about the plans for Carlton House. It was about *me me me*. I could identify Brummell's voice, and those of two or three other men with him. Brummell was making a reply to some remark:

"He asks me to advise him of his suits. I tell him he needs to make his lapels and pockets larger to compensate for his size and thus keep uniformity of shape; but he moans and laments that to do so only makes him look the larger. Thus he prefers to look instead like some child that's outgrown his skeleton suit."

"The Prince of Whales," said one, emphasising the H, "with so many tonnes of oil in his belly."

"One cannot trust a man who will not listen to good sense," said another.

"It is no easy task for me," said Brummell, "to make that man over in style, when he is so childish about the matter. A new idea every day, before the old fashion can even settle into the city! Alter the style too fast and it's not fashion, it's madness."

"They say that the mad are possessed with a special love for fine clothes," said one.

"And so ought the son of a madman, too."

There was a laugh. I was mortified by this; I could feel an inner sting as if tears would strike my eyes, but I swallowed deeply and fix'd my mind that it would not be permitted. Others in the hall could hear the insult too; a few of them looked at me with a sympathetic discomfiture. I considered whether to storm out of the house in resentment, but what a humiliating retreat that should be! So I calmed myself, and resolved that I should pay these gentlemen like insults in good time.

When Brummell's conference was over, I observed three well-clothed young men, all scarcely twenty years of age, emerge from the chamber. These visitors saw (and by the looks on their faces, recognized) me as soon as they stepp'd out. They greeted me affably, depicting no indication that they harboured either guilt or shame with regards to the things they had been saying about me just a few minutes prior. Likewise, I made no indication of having heard it.

Brummell saw me in the doorway and, with the offer of a smile and all the warmth and charm on earth, he invited me to come in directly. I insisted that he must first introduce me to his young friends; and this he did without hesitation. As it was, I should have known them already: one was the new Baron Alvanley, the next the Baron Byron, and the other Sir Henry Mildmay. Ah! Here was Brummell, bringing up the next generation of fops!

"It is an honor to meet you, sir," declared Byron to me. "I only ever saw you before at presentation."

With my head high and haughty, I sneered at him, for I still held *in petto* all my outrage. "I am sure that you did not dare to call me the fat Prince of *Whales* then," I answered.

The youths suddenly began to quiver back from me, dreading what I might do to them now that I was known to have overheard their prior insults. I could see the color draining from their handsome little faces.

Brummell hasten'd to step in on their behalf. "Aw, Prinny, you know how we all joke. Why, just yesterday we let Apollo Raikes leave here in tears after berating him for his dirty fingernails."

"You would think he had been putting his fingers up the a--- of a s--- leaking whore," said Byron, which obscene remark did produce shocked giggles from us all, myself there included.

Brummell was evidently pleas'd to see me smiling. "Here, Prinny: sit with us a while. I have a beautiful new snuff box, which I have been just dying to shew you." The Beau guided me to the best chair in the room, and gestured for his friends to sit down with me.

I was still stung by the remarks I had previously heard, but Brummell was now doing his best to lift my spirits. He called for his man to bring us all cherry brandy (my favourite drink) while he himself went to his cabinet to retrieve the box of which he had spoke.

Beau Brummell's snuff box collection was already becoming the stuff of legend; and over the years he would extend it greatly above what it was then. Snuff had been a longstanding fashion in England, but Brummell had refined it, as with every thing else. The box had to be disclosed with one hand, preferably without even glancing upon the contraption: only other people should look upon one's snuff box, but never the trinket's master. The same hand that had opened, was put to scoop a small quantity of the powder with the thumbnail, and it was then inhaled by the nose. A handkerchief was kept in the pocket to wipe away any unsightly brown smudges or drips. I myself always purposely lost my nail-full before it reached my nose: I did not enjoy tobacco, oh! but I loved the boxes.

Brummell now return'd to me, carrying a most delightful little snuff box formed in the shape of a turtle, fashioned in silver, with black Japanning on the shell. Oh! How could I remain in an ill temper, with such a darling sight before me? Brummell solicited me to use the treasure for the remainder of my visit, asserting that it was filled with an excellent blend from the town's best tobacconist. His little friends began to praise my choice of clothes and tailors, and by the time that I had intended to leave, I was in such a good humor that I gaily invited all of them to see me at the theatre that same evening, before I released them back out to their little lives.

Left there with Brummell, I supposed that I should see my visit done. I restored to him the little turtle box, but first I made a point to let him know, "The invitation extends to you, as well. I should be very glad to see you at the theatre."

"What is the shew?" he asked.

"I do not know, I am not going for the shew."

He agreed that he might attend. He understood my meaning; the theatre was to be but the start of an evening's carousing. It was without any question that I had situated myself into the position of the host, so if the night's enjoyment was to be on my bankbook, he was very glad to join.

"And what of the decorating at Carlton House?" I asked, for this had been the real purpose behind my visit that day.

"I have little news, for my appointments with every body are all intended for this morning," said he.

"Well, then I shall have to *insist* upon seeing you to-night, so that you may give me the report then."

Brummell agreed happily. I had already paid my necessary span of visitation, and so I left him at that time. As I went down the hall, on my way out of the door with the valet at my side, I could hear somebody curse me for having cut ahead of them in the queue. I told them to be d-----d. Did they not know who I was?

That same night, we fops all met at Drury Lane (the old theatre, before it burnt down.) Brummell sat in the box with me throughout the play, which we observed with disinterest. We spent more time in examination of the audience, through our golden lorgnettes. We admired or disparaged outfits worn by the populace of the better seats, marked who made a fine figure or who was too shabby to have merited leaving their own home. Wine was brought to us, which we enjoyed heartily. After the theatre we undertook the traditional occupation for the bucks about the town: a visit to one of the *maisons des debauches*. There are things one cannot bear to ask of dignified ladies, no matter how we might love them; and so we all resorted to the paid favours of these agreeable women of ill repute. It was a very regular pass-time for us gentlemen, in those days. The best brothels and bawdy houses were the ones farther to the west of the theatre, but one could sometimes find women more daring if one kept near to the stage. The main concern was that one had to mark whether any of the women from the house had been docked (that is, publicly shamed for having spread venereal diseases to one or more customers.) I kept well abreast of these matters, through my informants, and ensured that we only went to the best of establishments.

I never advertised my identity at any of the *stews*, as we call'd them; and if I was wearing my *Ich Dien* badge I always put it away before entering such a place; but there always seem'd to be an especial deference paid to me and to my companions, which implicated that the women were quite aware of just who was visiting, even when I sought to be *incognito*. Usually, a customer might sit for some drinks on the first floor, with a few of the available women, each of whom did all in her power to entice you to favour her above her sisters in arms; she might wear fewer clothes, pour more liquor or seek to speak more lubriciously. Rough men known as "bullies" might wait at hand to ensure the gentlemen visitors did not become too demanding or abusive at this point. Should one be desirous of some thing very particular, a word with the chief bawd might be in order, to make these special arrangements. In any event, there were normally rooms with couches or beds that each girl might keep for her own, and when one's companion for the evening was selected, you would retire with her to her own chamber.

The opening ceremony of choosing one's bedfellow was really where the best of the fun was, especially for a group. We gentlemen would be fought over by the women; we might squabble over some especially desirable beauty ourselves; we might even settle upon some unusual solution to our competition. Most of us bucks had lady friends in our lives already, some of us were even married; but it was the excitement of the selection that brought us to these ill-famed establishments time and again. Venereal desires filled the atmosphere, and for a small price one could be promised the delight of knowing their fulfillment, without any risque of disappointment.

CHAPTER 7.

Yelping of the Hounds

Some time later, I had occasion to dine with my brother, Frederick; the two of us were alone, and able to speak with perfect intimacy. I conceived it to be, therefore, my duty to inform him, of what I knew concerning the conduct of his wife. Although making every attempt to be gentle in my delivery of this bad news, I reported that I had been privy to some rumors concerning the Duchess, Frederica.

"What have you heard?" he asked, smiling in a skeptical manner.

"Do not take it too lightly," said I, "for I have reason to believe it is all true."

"What is it?" asked he, though I daresay not seeming so concerned as I would have expected.

"They say that Frederica has taken a lover," I answered.

"Well, that does not astonish me," said Frederick. "She is young enough, and must fulfill her passions somehow. I certainly will not do it for her."

I was surprized at this announcement. "Do you mean to say that you and Frederica have had a falling out?"

Frederick sipped his port with a more vivid interest than his tone suggested him to maintain for the subject of our conversation. "Dear George, we were scarcely ever *in* to begin with. It was an arranged match, just like you and Caroline. We do not really care that much for one another. I take my lovers, she takes hers. We have an agreement on it. Honestly, I am amazed only that it has taken so long for the matter to be discovered by you."

I was astonish'd, and also very dismayed. I had maintained a secret hope, for ages, that Frederick and Frederica would ensure the success of our Royal line. Now I found that it was to never be.

"Do you know what lover she has taken?" I ask'd, withholding any exhibition of my disappointment. "It is our friend the 'Beau' George Brummell."

Frederick did not display any signal of jealousy or dismay. "I am happy to hear that she does so well for herself," was his only answer, his tone conveying genuine gladness on his wife's behalf. "Every woman in London longs for that man's attentions, and I daresay, some of the men, too. She deserves a man of quality."

I was appall'd. "That clothes rack, a man of quality?"

"The women often stake their quality on that much, so why not the men?"

I groaned with disgust. "Do not tell me you have been reading that Wollstonecraft rubbish? But never mind it. Really, Frederick, I am aghast that you do not place a greater importance upon the dignity and honor of your wife."

He laughed in reply. "Dignity and honor! George, if we were to live that sort of life, we should simply follow father's instructions: no more drinking, shopping, racing, whoring, dancing or spending. Then what should we do with ourselves?"

"That is easy for you to say, you younger son," I answered with a mote of sarcasm. "You have no idea how disagreeable it is to have every politician in the country at your throat, demanding that you produce offspring, like some stud-horse!"

"Well, then, why do you not? Simply go to Caroline, do the deed, and you can cease to worry about it. Surely that is better than keeping yourself in this ill temper?"

"Ill temper!" I repeated, offended that he had so degraded the deepest feelings of my heart as a mere *temper*. Yet I had to acknowledge that he was wise in what he said.

Caroline was still at an age when what he proposed could be done. Perhaps the sacrifice of one more night with her would suffice to resolve my problems, rather than to keep myself fretting about these matters? Alas! If it were so, this meant that I should have to pay that detestable witch a visit.

***

Montagu House, at which Caroline resided, is a fine old house in a somewhat retired part of London. It was overcovered in ancient trees and vines which work'd together at hiding it away from the world. It was a perfect place to leave that b---h to be forgotten to time.

I did not announce my intention to visit: indeed, I told no one but my coachman of my intention to see her. It was my hope to find her at home during normal visiting hours. I was not disappointed: the steward announced me, with some amazement, and finally Caroline walked up to greet me with open arms and a great, drunken smile forced across her ugly German hussy face.

"George, dear!" she cried. "It has been ages. Whatever has brought you to visit, so unexpected?" Her voice, even beyond the distortions caused by her distinctly Germanic accent, was ragged and her speech a little slurred, as if she had been imbibing since morning.

Drinking was a favourite pass-time for her, at that point. "Had I known you were to come, I would have arranged the house for you. I know you like the chairs without arms."

I resolved to assume that she did not deliberately mean that as a jab about my weight. I paid her all due compliments and greetings, as if she were any other lady of quality, such as one who did not reek for twenty feet of onions. God, what did she do with onions, bathe in them? She invited me to sit on the couch with her, though we positioned ourselves about as far from one another as possible. Her clothing was of thick, heavy velvet, in a rather bizarre cut that looked almost theatrical. This was but one reason why I did not like to be seen at her side. But I was there to be amiable on that occasion, and I strove to overlook it.

"How is little William?" I asked, hoping only to make conversation by my inquiry.

She answered me, "He is well: he is visiting with some of his foster-siblings." The adopting of poor children had become a sort of a hobbyhorse for her. She had acquired over a half dozen since our marriage; well more than she could attend to by herself. William, to my knowledge, was the only one that actually lived at her house; and consequently there had been suspicions and rumors that he was secretly her own child, though these accusations had been quashed by an investigation. "Is this another interrogation?" she asked, alluding to that whole affair.

I sought to put her mind at ease. "Not at all," said I.

"And our Charlotte?" she asked.

I had not seen Charlotte in months. She was approximately ten years of age at this time, and lived almost wholly under the care of my parents, the King and Queen, but she did sometimes visit me at Carlton House, for I had the greater claim to her, as father. "She is well," I replied, pretending to know more than I did; but then, surely I would know of it were Charlotte any thing less than well. "You know you may visit her whenever you like…"

She replied without loss of her simper, "Under the scrutinizing eyes of all your family and watchdogs, ensuring that I behave myself becomingly…"

I groaned inwardly. She plainly harboured some desire to provoke an altercation. I had to reverse her on that course immediately. "Perhaps," said I, striving to be as diplomatic as I could, "we can minimize the need for it, by making a shew of just how well I trust you."

"What do you mean by this?" she asked, raising her eyebrow in doubt of my word.

"The fact is," said I, "I have come here to propose that we might see one another with a little more regularity. I think it might be good for us: for Charlotte, too."

The look of doubt did not leave her face. "Dear George, is Parliament threatening to take away your allowance again, if you will not produce them another heir?"

She was wrong on my motive, but seemingly had guessed of my intention. "Not at all," said I. "And yet, to the matter of another heir: perhaps it is a matter we might put under some consideration for the sake of —"

"Oh no," she said, bolting upright in her seat and seeming as if she would actually stand with outrage. "It was decided after our wedding night, after your mistress Lady Jersey sought to poison me with Epsom salt, after you went senselessly drunk on the floor of our bedchamber and slept there the night —"

"Obviously I did manage to perform some thing," I grumbled, "for Charlotte attests to that."

"The ticking of the clock counted less than a minute of work from your end, during the whole of which I feared that you might vomit over me."

I sneered at her. "*Two* minutes; do not strive to insult me by cutting down the numbers more than what they were. You are lucky I was able to endure so much as that. You did not exactly arrive from the continent in the cleanest condition. I know that there they think a wedding bouquet is sufficient to cover the stench from lack of bathing."

"Perfume is no substitute for a bath, George," she said pointedly. "Has not your friend Brummell taught you any thing?"

Brummell! I found the name to sting. Why did it? Why should it? Was he not a friend of mine? Yet my heart reacted as if bitten. "What do you know of Brummell's bathing?" asked I.

"Every body knows of Brummell's bathing ritual. I have attended his morning shew of it just like every one else in this city."

I was appalled. "You call upon him at his house, and watch him bathe?"

It was this sort of immodest behavior that had compelled the late investigation into her conduct, though while it was certainly indecent and unbecoming for her to undertake such activities, there was no *legal* barrier to it.

"I am a married woman," she answered. "What harm is it? I think it more suspicious that *you* took an interest in watching another man to bathe himself. Who are you, Edward the Second?" The woman was making my blood boil. "Besides, it is not as if I am in the tub with him as he goes about it; I know only what I see reflected in his dressing mirror, from outside the door. 'Twas you who popularized that shew; it is a shame that you have not learnt from it. You knew him then."

"I know him *now*," I said, affronted by a suggestion in her tone that I was not presently an intimate friend to this man of fashion. "And did you know what he was about these days, you might not regard him quite so highly."

"Why, George! Do I detect rightly, that you are envious of him? Brummell never does wrong, except in the eyes of a jealous rival for his place. The women are practically boxing one another for the chance at him." She smiled with an artificial succor. "Sweet George, is that it? Are the women leaving off of you for him? You cannot blame them: he is young, and handsome: and his influence is nearly equal to your own —"

"Oh, enough on that infernal Brummell!" cried I. "I am not here for his sake, but for ours."

"For *yours*, dear George," said she. "I have no need of you, for sure; so what is your use for me?"

I had come that day because my pride was on the line, the fate of the monarchy was on the line: and yet, after ten minutes' talk with her, I could foresee no help or improvement to be gained towards either purpose. While there was plenty at stake, I certainly was not going to stoop to beg for her vile favours: I could let the House of Hanover fall with a much easier heart than I could degrade myself for the sake of this trash. In lieu any answer I stood up, and without a word I walked from the room. I needed nothing from a sluttish hussy such as she. I could hear her laugh behind me as I went out the door.

CHAPTER 8.

Who Wears a Garment Shapeless and Unfinished?

Brummell was not entirely effeminate in his skills; he could both shoot and ride, but he did not display any significant fondness for either of these talents. *In primus*, he did not like to rise early enough in the day to join a morning hunt; but he reported to me that his greatest obstacle to finding pleasure in these tasks, was that he could not bear to have his boots and clothing splashed by the mud when riding about the countryside.

When the war against Napoleon was renewed, the Duke of Rutland had raised a corps of volunteers to guard the coast against any threat of invasion. As Brummell had once been a soldier in my regiment, and was at that time staying in the area for the season, Rutland gave him a

Majority. (Perhaps this was an effort to provide a hard-up Brummell with some kind of respectable income, but I only speculate.) In any event, Brummell was prevailed upon to accept the position. In the course of the general inspections of the volunteer corps, an Officer was sent from the Horse Guards to review the Duke's regiment, the Major being in command. On the day of the inspection, every one was on parole except the Major-Commandant. The Officer was incensed, but Major Brummell could not be found. The inspection proceeded, and when it was near its close, there at full gallop across the country, in the uniform of the Belvoir Hunt, was Brummell. He was terribly splashed with mud and grime. He apologized and sought to explain his tardiness by the report that, having departed from Belvoir Castle quite early, he had expected to be on the parade in time, the meet being close at hand; however, his favourite horse had suffered an accident, in consequence of which he had been tossed into a ditch, and he had required much time to recover himself. Even though it must have been a terrible accident indeed that should have compelled the fastidious Brummell to ever let himself be seen in so dirtied a condition, the Officer was not moved to any pity by this explanation.

"Sir," he said, quite livid with rage, "this conduct is wholly inexcusable. If I remember right, sir, you once had the honor of holding a Captain's commission under his

Royal Highness the Prince of Wales, sir! Now, I tell you that I should be wanting in the proper zeal for the honor of the service: I should be wanting sir, if I did not this very evening report this disgraceful neglect of orders to the Commander in Chief, as well as the state in which you present yourself in front of your regiment; and this shall be done sir. You may retire, sir."

All this was very solemn and upsetting; but Brummell's presence of mind was not often upset. He bowed in acknowledgement of the reproof, but had scarcely walked his horse a few paces from the spot, when he returned and said in a subdued tone, arching his eyebrows mischievously:

"Excuse me, General; but in my anxiety to explain this most unfortunate business, I forgot to deliver a message from the Duke of Rutland. It was to request the honor of your company at dinner."

The faces of both men brightened at once. The Officer coughed, and cleared his throat sufficiently to express his thanks. "Ah! Why, really, I feel and am very much oblig'd to his Grace. Pray, Major Brummell, tell the Duke I shall be most happy." He then spoke again at full volume: "Major Brummell, as to this little affair, I am sure no man can regret it more than you do. Assure his Grace, that I shall have great pleasure in accepting his very kind invitation." They parted amid a shower of smiles.

Brummell had yet but half completed his performance; for the invitation was his own invention, and he found that he was obliged to gallop posthaste to Belvoir, to acquaint Rutland of the guest he was to receive on that day. Such was Mr. Brummell's cleverness and influence over every body.

I should own that I *was* envious of Brummell. Whilst he passed two hours washing each day, to the delight of all that observed him, I spent nearly as much time stuffing myself into a glorified pair of stays, and a yoke to force my chin up. His slim torso flattered any cut of suit he dreamt of, whilst I had to have mine cut in deference to my shape. But it was more than that: he had the looks, the life, the influence, and moreover the love of people that I had so desired for myself. Yet Brummell knew nothing of my feelings towards him. Why should he? I had not said any thing. In fact, he still trusted me dearly as one of his closest friends. That was why he soon came to visit me at Carlton House, with the intention of requesting a favour from his dear old Prinny.

He was not the only person who had morning levées. On occasion he would make an appearance at mine, though this more often back in his teens, when he was still in my service. Still, on this morning he arrived, all aged in his twenties; and I receiv'd him with the utmost courtesy, despite that my levées were normally reserved for gentlemen of a higher station than he. Brummell's fashionability, as ever, conferred him special privilege. He sat across from me in my closet, his long buckskin-clad legs arranged in a comfortable posture. As he surveyed my preparation for the day, he wore a docile countenance; sheepish, even. I was being put into my shirt. The high collar required a procedure to adjust into the correct design, one which the two of us had perfected so many years past. The collar was, at first, so tall that one's face was almost completely covered by it: the valet or assistant needed to fold it down and tuck it in place, after which the nearly as tall cravat was wrapped into position, and by a repeated opening and closing of the jaw it was forced downways to fit. Brummell himself came forward to assist me with the final decorative folds and knots.

"Well done, Prinny! You have not lost the knack," said he, using a new handkerchief to crease the cravat so as not to smudge it with any finger-dirt.

"I invented it: I ought to know how to do it," I answered.

Whilst he fumbled about the area of my neck, he happened upon the black ribband that supported Maria's portrait. "What is this nasty thing?" he ask'd, seeing only the ribband. Flustered, I told him it was no business to him and not to touch it; and at that, he left off the matter. It was not in his interest to upset me to-day. I tucked the ribband out of all sight, and proceeded.

"Well, Brummell," said I, "to what do I owe this pleasure? It has been so long since you came to visit that I was beginning to fear you had forgot me."

"Aw, I could never forget my dear Prinny," said he, with his usual drawling tone. "It is simply that the people in this city keep me so preoccupied. I have visitors from morning till night; I scarcely have time enough to even dress between meals."

"The high cost of popularity," said I.

"Indeed, sir. But I shall discover my real purpose; I did not come for a mere friendly visit myself. I have come to you, my old friend, in need of some assistance."

I demonstrated concern for him, and induced him to tell me more, so I could offer whatever aid was in my power. At this time, three valets began the procedure of wrapping me into my prison of whalebone, and of pulling the cords as near together as they could get.

Brummell colored a bit at what he next said, though whether it was from shame for his circumstance or discomfort at seeing my painful lacing procedure, I cannot tell. "The fact is, your Royal Highness," said he, "the fortunes of the card table have not been, lately, kind to me. I have incurr'd some debts: nothing beyond my means to repay, of course, but the moneylenders are becoming rather impatient with me."

I groaned slightly as the valets began to tighten the cords about me. "Do you mean to say that you require a loan?"

"Aw, nothing so vulgar as that," said Brummell. "Why, I could hie to the pawnbroker with any snuff box or pocket-watch I have, were some money all that I needed."

"Then what do you suppose I can do for you?"

He was grave as he spoke. "I need your clout," he said. "I need only your word, to the moneylenders, that you trust me. You have trusted me, have you not? All I need is for you to convey that trust to Mr. Gibbs, so he will leave off. I am certain that my fortunes soon shall improve, and I will be able to repay every thing in full; I only need time, but it is time that my creditors do not wish to bestow."

"Does the E S Q you append to your name not suffice?"

"Evidently not. To be a gentleman, does not pay."

"What does, then?"

He smiled reassuringly. "My friends take good care of me; I never pay for an evening's entertainment, and I receive so many gifts of furniture and clothing I have but few expenses there. It is just for little things, like my servants, my house, my memberships at the clubs. My annuities will pay out in a few more months, but just until then… if your Royal Highness will condescend to grant me his favour…"

I admit, I liked the way that he pleaded for my help. I returned his smile, even as I was trapped in an awkward posture whilst I was being bound up tighter and tighter.

"You need not fear. I will do whatever I can for you. Do not worry anymore about those moneylenders: I will see to it that they know how well I trust you, that I am backing you; and that you are worthy to receive their trust in turn."

Brummell thanked me most graciously for my promise. He remained to watch that my belt was fitted becomingly, and then departed as soon as my morning face-leeches were applied, this being a little more than he could bear the sight of. Nevertheless, we parted ways in the happiest of spirits. It seem'd to me that Brummell had been humbled by his circumstance; and that was all that I had truly desired from him. We were back at the understanding of just who was the master and who was the lackey. I was Prince: he was my subject, and thus it ever would be. I was glad to make it known to the moneylenders and bankers that Brummell was under my protection, and should be left undisturbed.

CHAPTER 9.

Another Flap-Mouthed Mourner

My sister, Amelia, was seven and twenty at the time of her death. She had been in poor health for many years beforehand: consumption, erysipelas, rheumatism, she bore it all. It was therefore not entirely a surprize that she succumb'd to this tragic turn. Notwithstanding this, she was my youngest sibling, and it was a sad day for every body when she passed on to her greater rewards in the next world. I requested to have a death mask, to remember her by.

Grievously touched as were all of us, her siblings, by her death, my father's grief was beyond all measure. It was more than grief: it was mania. His famed madness was often aggravated by any heightened emotion, and this was indeed a very sharp blow to him, enough to provoke the most antick behavior and bring every body to the greatest concern for him. I shall confess, we had not seen him so bad since the year eighty-eight, when he had been oblig'd to retire from London for the first time in his life, to the spa at Cheltenham, so as to purge the malign humors which afflicted him. He had been unable to open the Parliament that year. It became necessary for the Lords to go forward without him, and I was chosen to act as Regent in his place: though my father recovered himself before it had become necessary for me to take any action, and ultimately every thing resumed as it ever was.

Yet there had been, I perceived, a change in the public's attitude toward me after that past event. To acknowledge the reality, long-established tho' it was, that I might one day be King, seem'd to discomfit a good many people. It soon became apparent that I was far from beloved by certain venomous persons. Under their influence, every body began to loathe me; to hate me. How I struggled from that point forward to make myself so likeable and agreeable! I sought to keep myself occupied: but with my father, the King, running the country, and my brother Frederick in command of the military, there was little of national consequence for me to do. The shameful crime of marrying Caroline was about as much as was demanded of me. So it was to Art and Beauty I devoted myself. Who does not love Beauty? These politicians, evidently! Rarely a kind word could I expect from their mouths. They compared me to Nero and Caligula, saying that I squandered the country's wealth on luxury during a time of need. For twenty years I had been able to look past it, for the most part, (*les fous se mêlent de tout*) but with my Royal father's illness having struck him out of service once again, the past precedent was looked to, and it was apparent that I should once again be called upon to act as Regent.

I was not granted even a moment to enjoy my new status. Immediately the pamphlets, the papers, the magazines began to speak out against me. *"A sovereign has much to learn, and much to perform — but the education of princes, radically wrong, seems, even after the terrible misfortunes which have resulted from a system as absurd as pernicious, to have made little impression upon the common sense of mankind; empires descend to the next in succession with less conditions annexed to them than an entailed estate, and are seized upon as an inheritance by the fool or knave in succession, without an idea of any responsibility to God or man being annexed to the inheritance. Away with the profligate servility that destroys royalty, while it pretends to worship it; that denies that it has duties to perform, or obligations to discharge, and maintains contrary to experience, that it is as secure from infamy and reproach as it is from the gibbet. Born in a luckless hour for themselves and for the people whom they impoverish and misrule — with intellects barely sufficient to know they can be vicious with impunity, their crimes are without provocation and their arrogance without dignity. Sovereignty, burlesqued by their folly and rendered odious by their guilt, is degraded in the public opinion, with little chance of regaining the respect it has forfeited. With nothing more of royalty belonging to them than its pageantry, the fall of such men can neither excite wonder nor commiseration. Their career through life is known only by the waste they occasion, and the progress of the snail is traced by its slime; and, as they have lived despised, they die unlamented."* This was all in a publicly published work entitled *A Letter to His Royal Highness the Prince of Wales*! Then there were the awful questions: why had I abandoned Caroline, why did I not produce an endless line of offspring with her? How dare I ignore the holy sanctity of marriage, leaving my poor ugly German wife locked up in Montagu House while I dwelt separately within the same city? And good God, how the public sided with that teutonic Xanthippe! She had kept so well to herself, that they had not formed any negative images of her. They remembered only the splendour of our marriage ceremony, and the happy event of Charlotte's birth, and in that favourable portrait she was for ever posed for them. I could have died in my agony.

***

Superfine wool is a lovely material: soft textured, very thin, with a bit of a sheen to it, however, not so smooth as silk. It is my preferred cloth for a modern coat. I like Royal blue for my color: it is more festive than dreary black, which is what Brummell prefers and has settled upon the land as fashion. But Brummell has the preference. A trifle the preference.

So we overheard at Schweitzer's one day, when we came in, unannounced, on an extempore shopping voyage. Brummell knew that I lov'd to shop, and apparently having found me so disspirited of late, he requested the honor of my company on one of his own excursions. *Impromptu*, we had thought to order new coats, and had come to the shop without ceremony. We discovered, within, some wealthy foreigner; who was to all appearance looking to become a man of fashion, and had ask'd to be fitted in the height of English style. Schweitzer himself was not in the room: an apprentice helped the man in his selection, and bade the gentlemen choose a fabric for his new coat. The foreigner deferr'd to the tradesman: what should he suggest?

"Why sir," was the answer, "the Prince wears superfine, and Mr. Brummell the Bath coating. Suppose sir, we say Bath coating; *I think Mr. Brummell has a trifle the preference.*"

The tailor's assistant was so engrossed in this business that he had not marked our entry or that the two very figures of which he spoke had entered the shop, and were in fact observing his lessons on fashion. I concealed my dismay at what he spoke by accusing, to Brummell, that the apprentice knew nothing of fashion or of trends or of us, but inside I was stung by his hearty assurance that Brummell was the man to follow. For Heaven's sake, I *made* Brummell. Now *he* was my superior in fashionability? All in black, like some lawyer or clergyman? In that rough, nappy Bath coating? I think that Brummell perceived my agitation over this the conversation we had heard *par hasard*, for he soon suggested that we should leave the shop and allow our foreign friend to conduct his business; there were ample opportunities to shop elsewhere on this same road. *C'était bien par moi.*

Footmen were outside to carry away any goods we procured, and my man John scurried after me with a bag of money, to pay the merchants for my purchases. The retinue followed us to and fro as we made our way about. The street was trimmed on both sides with plenty of places for two gentlemen of means to buy their way out of boredom. Each little purchase was a trophy, some new delight to admire. At my house were rooms full up with clothes and baubles, many that I had never even used, but to shop for more always seem'd to cheer me somewhat, and to make me feel accomplish'd. The beautiful items were mine and I was ever glad to acquire more.

Working our way to another shop that sold fine jewelry, my eye was caught by their display case of finger rings; by the time we left I had bought three of them. Brummell had in the meantime added another item to his famous snuff box collection. The card tables must have been kind to him, I thought.

As we left the shop to visit the next, the two of us walking side by side, a young gentleman of perhaps fifteen or sixteen years approached us. He shewed all signs of having recognized our identities, and behaved toward us with as profound a reverence as can be safely displayed on a public street. Not so rude as to introduce himself, he merely greeted us and paid wordy compliments to our manner of dress. We tipped our hats to him. He began to ask of us what it would take for a lad like himself to be so finely attired. Brummell made the answer, and I think he felt every genuine desire to be encouraging to this youth when he replied: "With strict economy, I am sure you could do it for about £800* a year!"

Plainly, the young man was alarmed by such a gargantuan number. "£800 a year? My entire allowance for that time is but £200."

"Do not allow that to hinder you," said Brummell. "To live within one's means displays a lack of imagination. Spend: and God will provide!"

The young man thanked Brummell, and went on his way with a cheerful attitude. Brummell then leaned in towards me and spoke.

---

* Present day equivalency is estimated at about £60,000.

"I neglected to tell him the real secret," said he. "Play c--kmonger to a woman with ample money."

That made me laugh, for indeed that seemed to be the means by which we gentlemen of fashion were obliged to settle debts. "Don't let any body say that we do not work for it."

We proceeded to a cloth merchant, where we were dazzled by such nice and lovely and radiant materials, that I simply *had* to buy some. Brummell raised his eyebrows at my purchase of a bolt of yellow silk brocade.

"What on earth will you do with that, Prinny?"

"I am not yet certain," said I. "Perhaps a waistcoat?"

"A waistcoat of that! Oh no, Prinny, are you reverting to the middle ages? Taking us back to the Norman invasion?"

"Perhaps a dressing gown, then," I grumbled, my enthusiasm dimming in the face of his disapprobation. "I simply admired the material."

"Aw, Prinny, they already call you the *Prince of Whales*. The last thing you need right now is to get yourself compared to a b----y pineapple. Remember: simplicity! The entire Grecian ideal is based on the elegance of *simplicity!*"

"But maybe we do not need to restrict the fashion to simplicity all of the time."

"Good taste is good taste; fashion influences it only so much."

"Have you not seen depictions of the way that the beaux dressed a hundred years gone? Surely they thought it looked well enough at the time."

"Aw, that was but evidence of decay reaching its utmost; the men looked like women, the women like lobsters. In the century since, we have come to understand the value of simplicity of dress, just as the Greeks understood it."

"I think if we took up an exact copy of the Greeks, we gentlemen should find ourselves with more exposed legs than are presently deemed fit for public view."

"The 'unmentionables' are made to mimick that," said Brummell, using the learned term for the style of tight trousers he wore. For my part I donned them but rarely, preferring my knee-breeches, which I thought more formal and more flattering since, alas! I will own it: my legs were a little too wide to look handsome in the long leggings that Brummell had made *un nouvelle mode*.

"I am not built for Grecian modes, these days," said I.

"Really, what you might do best with (if you would make yourself more fashionable) is to take Lord Byron's example and leave off eating a meal or so each day. He has been fighting with his girth, as well."

"You are not so slim as you once were, either," I said, not without some bitterness attending my tone. He understood my intended insult, but bore it with a confounded grace.

"Aw, I had to dismiss my cook, for I so rarely eat at home; I am ask'd to a dozen dinners, teas and suppers each day. It is natural; and I am certain that your Royal Highness is every bit as much in demand to bestow his company to the best people in this city. To overindulge naturally leads to some crimes against beauty. We merely have to keep ourselves in check."

Good Lord, my father used to say such manner of things to me. I recalled how he used to restrict my diet: denying me the best foods or portions of meals, in an effort to keep me slim and handsome as his ideal heir ought to be, in his mind (his crazed mind.) I thanked Brummell for his well-intentioned advice and secretly wish'd to wring his skinny little neck.

"Come, Prinny: let us go promenade. It is almost five o'clock."

Together we went to the park, riding in my carriage. On promenade I walked at his side, but I was like a mere shadow to the sparkling figure of Beau Brummell, despite the mighty gleam of my insignia badge. I bore the inattention decently, but inside, I fumed. Every man there was in *my* high collar, *my* side-whiskers, *my* Hessians, and yet

116

they behaved as if I were a leper, bestowing only polite nods to "your Highness" but none of the affectionate regard which was showered upon the sage Brummell, who had merely popularized my inventions. The few men who did wish to speak to me sought only to talk of politics, as if I were some kind of Minister. Somewhere in the depths of my heart I could *sense* that I should be able to look as good as Brummell. What element evaded me, what secret of the art? When I had begun to associate with him, it was with hope that he could better me; but now he did so much more than that. He did not better me but rather had *bested* me. My patronage had empowered him more than it had operated to my own benefit. *Come la man mi pizzica! Che smania, che furor! Come il polmon mi si altera! Che smania, che calor!*

At length, the display ended, and I saw Brummell back to his home. The Beau left with a smile and a few more kind words of encouragement for me. He always was sympathetic towards those whom he perceived as being used unfairly, just like in his Eton days. I bade him farewell, feeling disgusted with myself and hating the man for having caused *me* to feel so.

CHAPTER 10.

A Dying Coal Revives with Wind

Talk of a Regency advanced, and it was apparent that I needed to retaliate against a negative public image. I had to present my best face to the public, and shew to them that I was capable of acting the wise and virtuous leader that was desired to govern them. A fresh view of me had to be presented, a new fashion set. I knew the man who could advise me best on it; and so, I called for Mr. Brummell to attend me as soon as possible, to provide his ever worthy sartorial advice. He may have looked bleak for my taste, but all the world adored his final *ensembles*.

To my great surprize and dismay, *soon as possible* did not come soon. After weeks, I made an inquiry as to Mr. Brummell's condition. I was inform'd that he was not even in London; he was in Nottinghamshire, at the country home of his friend Lord Byron.

Byron had been a part of the Beau's set for a while; but it was only lately that the young Baron had come into his own notoriety. He had recently returned from travels in the orient, full of interesting stories to tell: but moreover, he had published some volumes of poetry, which were becoming known and talked about all over the English-speaking world. Brummell's *protegés* were blossoming into bright celebrities in their own right.

I sent word to Byron's property, the medieval Newstead Abbey, and I receiv'd from my servant the report that it had become a haven for the *beau monde*. Every fashionable person of consequence, or person who had pretensions to become so, look'd to have an invitation to Newstead Abbey, now that it was under Brummell's directives in its renovation and the character of its entertainments. The parties which were held at the Abbey, I am told, might have been a little too extravagant, even *outré*, for the usual London crowd of matrons and politicians. They were more what one would expect of Trimalchio than of John Bull. Yet with such a man as Byron as host, it was surely not to be any subtle or quiet affair. The wine and spirits flowed freely, as it always must, but there it was served by female waiters dressed in men's livery, their legs and buttocks on display, masked only by the fabric of the breeches. At the dinner, an astounding twelve courses were served, each dish a work of art in its presentation as much as in its preparation. Byron knew a magnificent French chef, who made every effort and exertion for the accomplishment of his dishes, and who must have had a team of angels whispering inspirations to him, for he concocted such fantastical delights! There was white soup seasoned and colored lavender, beef with foie gras and truffles, cakes with chocolate in them, *etc. etc. etc.* O Genius! I would have hired him away for myself, had he been willing to retire from Byron's service. Then to give pleasure to the heart as well as the stomach, every room of the ancient castle was filled with some sort of delight. Brummell had overseen the decoration, putting the walls and furnishings into his signature bold but almost Spartan stylings. Upon passage through each door, one did find endless entertainments: there was a room inside which a candle burnt, that had some occult ability to create illusions and visions of spirits in its shadows: in another were a complete troupe of acrobats, performing away: another room where unusual liquors such as laudanum, cannabis oil and satyrion were distributed, for those revellers who found the usual champagnes and brandies too ordinary for such an event. You can well guess what effect such libations, alone or in combination, had upon the minds of the guests. It was farrago and nonsense: like living in a ballet rather than attending a mere party! And of course there was musick: any musick one might like. Dances were in one place, folk melodies in another, a formal quartet playing serenades in another. And the people in attendance! The presence of Brummell and Byron by themselves could have fixed the success of any revelry, but every beau, rake, author, actor, painter, courtesan, wit, inventor, dancer, philosopher and bluestocking was there, in perfect harmony with one another and their surroundings. The conversations that must have happened there: I die with envy at the thought of them! I was told the names of those who attended, and would you believe it? Every fashionable name in England was there. The only person missing was H. R. H. the Prince of Wales.

Naturally I inquired with the Corinthians as to why I was not amongst the Newstead Abbey's crowd. I was inform'd that the group was of a mob of one mind who were looking to break away from the politically charged climate of London, and that with the renewed talk of a Regency, it was only natural that I should *not* be included in their pleasure parties, which existed wholly for the sake of beauty; that is to say, my presence and society might be upsetting to them and embarrassing to their intent of knowing pure pleasure. The excuse was dismaying to me, but at the time it did sound sensible enough. The state of politics was looking very bleak, and I should have lik'd to escape it as much as any body. I could see why those who were able to do it, did so. Yet for me, it was no option. I had to speed my way to somehow improving my public image. The most hurtful cartoons were being printed about me each day: there was one which actually depicted me as a big, fat whale, blowing favours out from my nostrils. (Is there any need for me to explain the pun?) A bare-breasted mermaid that suspiciously resembled Maria was drawn at my side. I wrote desperately to Brummell and asked that if he could not return to London to see me, that he should at least write me with his good advice. I receiv'd a reply, in which he merely promis'd to return to London soon, at which time he wou'd examine the matter with me in person. Till then, I was *seulet*.

As I sat one evening, alone (for the furor surrounding me had brought me to disdain company in a manner that I had never before known) I occupied myself by playing upon my cello. I am, in fact, a tolerably good cellist. The ancient Pharaohs and Caesars would have clapped their hands and demanded musicians come out to play a tune for them; but I contented myself with my own musick. I was learning a piece by Beethoven, viewing the sheet musick by candlelight, in my own chamber. While I was well occupied with my endeavors to hear the tune in my head, I became distracted by a small commotion that was forming outside of the house: voices shouting, not too numerous, but perhaps as if five or six men were involved in a disagreement or altercation of some sort. I went to the window to see what the commotion was for, but from my spot I could not view the cause for it. I decided to go downstairs to investigate the matter. I meant to find one of my servants to have him tell me what was about, but as it was, I discovered they were all in search of me.

"What is happening outside?" I asked my steward.

"Your Highness, it is evidently his Majesty your father."

I was alarmed to hear that. "Has he been shewn in?" I asked.

"We are attempting to coax him in," was the reply. "The guards do not dare to touch him." I was dismayed: I recognized that these words meant he had wandered over here in the midst of some fit of madness. There was no use asking why he wanted to see me: the answer would likely remain just as mysterious, even if it were known, to people possessed of reason.

I confirmed that word had been already sent to St. James about his whereabouts, and then with my steward at my side, I went out to witness his condition. I could see him, a few of my servants about him, as well as a couple more whose livery marked that they had chased after him from the palace. My Royal father was clad only in his nightshirt: but I was relieved that at least he was dressed in *some thing*, for I have heard that on previous occasions he had been known to roam off from his rooms completely nude. He was staggering about the pathway before the house in the moonlight, plainly confused for where he was. He must have walked the half-mile from St. James in that condition. I was terribly humiliated, flustered, and alarmed by the entire circumstance.

I hurried over to him, poor old man, and I addressed him with a heavy heart. "Sir!" I called, "please, let us get you inside the house."

My father recognized me, I could see in his face. "George," he said, proceeding to my side, "I am so glad to have found you at last for I have been looking for you for so long and I have wanted to find where you were and luckily I find you now so I can tell you all of the beautiful plans that I have for you which you will love, and it will be so exciting for us both to see the fruition of all that I have devised and you will love it for I have been looking for you for quite a while now..." *et caetera*. He talks a great deal when he becomes like this, and all very swiftly so that one can scarce understand a word of it. It matters little whether it is understood, since one is lucky if even half of it makes sense. I, along with several other footmen and valets, guided him into the house whilst we awaited a carriage and some extra hands to come to take him home. I busied him in the doorway by forcing myself to listen to his jumble of words, degrading as it was for me. He started to ramble and rave, declaring some story about me, as a baby, (this in front of all these servants, who to their credit kept straight faces through it all.)

The nightmare worsened as we waited: he began to tell me of some great scheme he had for my betterment. It involved dressing myself as a pig. He began to misremember my nickname of Prinny as *Piggy* and he repeatedly called me by this. Any other man on earth I would have boxed on the ears by this time. I looked continually to the door, very anxiously, to see whether the carriage was ready to take him back to the palace.

Finally he got around to the crux of whatever scheme he envisioned for whatever purpose his mind had deemed important. He declared that he had selected a new wife for me, that she was a tea-cup. I checked and checked again that this was not some unfamiliar cant term, but he confirm'd to me he meant a literal cup used for serving tea: he had found an especially beautiful one which he earnestly desired I should marry. At that time the carriage was finally ready for him, thank heavens, and all of the servants together were able to rush and tackle him, to carry him away, (he appearing quite bewildered at his condition.) For my part, I was in tears by the end of it: woeful, wretched tears of utter frustration. All the while my brain twisted round and round the consideration of this horrifying fact: that my Royal father was presently a more beloved monarch than me, it was he that the people did not wish to see replaced, and I seem'd to be incapable of exceeding even his amazingly low-set bar.

I called for my valet. "Bring some brandy up to my chamber," I commanded through sniffles. I was in need of the greatest cheer I could provide myself. "And also, bring in all of my erotic snuff boxes."

"Yes, your Highness."

The miniature nude scenes and burning brandy became my companions as I played cello into daybreak, stopping only when I had had too much drink to be capable of holding the bow any longer.

***

Life cannot be but work alone. There must be time for amusements. My favourite place to find them, is at Brighton, formerly called Brighthelmstone. I have gone there during summer, at frequent and regular intervals, since about the time that I married Maria. At the onset, it was but a scheme devised by me in order to hide myself away from my father; but I discovered this happy place to be possessed of such boundless charm, and so enjoyable, that I continu'd to return year after year. I built a Pavilion and stables for my use. By my influence and patronage, what had formerly been a quiet seaside village became a favourite retreat for the *ton* of London. The yearly racing was perhaps the main attraction. One of my life's finest moments was at the Brighton Races, in the year 1805. The year previous, I had purchased an exceedingly fine stud horse named Orville, from one Mr. Wilson. This beautiful beast, I entered into the race that year. It was done on a lark: I did not really expect him to win, and in fact it was to be my duty that year to present a trophy to whatever person *did* own the winning animal.

When the race began, several other horses went to the lead; but in the final moments, Orville took the inside track and flew to the foremost spot. He won the race in a feat that had all of the crowd crying out with excitement and celebration.

Naturally I ought to have been the recipient of the trophy, but I could not very well award it to myself. I thus gave it over to Mr. Wilson, who was in attendance. I was happy to do it, for the trophy meant little to me: it was the applause, and the cheers from the enthusiastic crowd, that fitted me with the utmost delight, and which still gladden my heart even now as I recall them to memory.

Yet the strains under which I laboured by the year 1811 were coming to take a great toll upon me, and even the mirth of Brighton seemed inadequate to relieve my sorrows during this unhappy time of my burgeoning Regency.

In that town, there were more than only the formal horse races: along the Brighton Road there were also matches of a less refined nature, held between gentlemen on horseback or in phaetons. I lik'd to participate, as a form of exercise; and certainly my equipment in terms of phaetons and horses was without rival. It was granted that I could not win every race, even at that; but zounds! I did give them a challenge.

It was as I pouted from a lost race on the road, which I daresay I felt had been unfairly called (the young man who had beaten me, I am sure, had started prematurely; but nobody else had made note of it) when I notic'd that my breath seem'd to fall short. I began to clutch at my chest and feel exceedingly light-headed. I was forc'd to excuse myself, and retire to my home, the Pavilion, in my weakened state. I scarcely made it through the door. My servants hurri'd to help me to my bed.

Physicians were called for, and upon their examination of me I was determin'd to suffer from nerves and fever, provoked by my late strains and exhaustion. The usual treatments were given to me, and I was instructed to keep to my bed till such time as I should be well and fully restor'd to health. This advice was taken, frankly without any need to compel me, for I did not feel well enough to attempt any thing much to the contrary. I laid weak and miserable for the next several days, struggling to console myself with juleps and with an illustrated edition of *Les Bijoux Indiscrets*. My friends were scattered all over the country, going about their own businesses, so I had few visitors, and I was left much to my loneliness for most of the time: the only visits I receiv'd were from governmental Ministers, whose presence I would never be freed from again for the rest of my life, I am unhappy to own. I wrote word to a few of my friends and family, to inform them of my condition, but the bulk of my time was spent supine amongst my pillows, in a dizzy fog of medicines and fainting that seemed as if it might never relent, and would turn itself into one more burden to last throughout my sorry life.

Such a dejection had continued for about a week, until such a day (O what a happy day!) that an utter miracle took place, an event which brought such consolation and rejoicing that I never would have dared to hope for it. I receiv'd a most special visitor, one I could have never been brave enough to expect: it was

Maria! Maria! Maria!

My heart leapt to a happy dance within my breast the moment that I heard her name. She had been in Brighton, and having been notified by my brother Frederick that I was unwell, she had condescended to visit her poor, half-dead spouse during what might be his final days. She was lovely as ever as she entered my chamber, dressed beautifully and tastefully, *cheveux bien coiffés*, and just a smudge of cosmetic enhancing her pretty complexion.

"Maria," I said to her, my eyes sparkling with tears of happiness, my blood warmly racing for what seemed like the first time in ages, "if any thing can induce me to live, it is surely your visit."

Maria took a seat by the bed, and squeezed my hand in hers, smiling with *un grand sentiment.* "You never fall ill when you're in Brighton," she said. "I perceived that this illness must be genuine."

Maria always was rather too honest in her assessments of me; but at this time I could forgive virtually any thing from her. I call'd for wine to be brought to us while we visited, and then I sent away the servants. By nightfall, Maria was still at my side, but now in the bed with me, admiring the scar on my breast from when I had stabbed myself on her behalf, all those years before. She express'd amazement that I still kept her picture around my neck every day. I was so happy to be in her arms again! We were both older and fatter than we had ever been before, but when is one not? She stayed on at the Pavilion for many days, her official purpose being to nurse me back to health. Simply to have her with me again was all that I needed in order to feel better than ever. We were soon reconciled, entwined in a perfect adoration and contentment with one another. As always, we could not really live together thanks to that Brunswickan harpy back in London; but Maria and I were once again united as a couple, the happy couple we ought to have been for all those years. It was as if a new life had been breathed into me, and I promised myself, silently, that I would not spoil things with her ever again. This time I would be impeccable, and I would maintain her love using every thing that was in my power.

CHAPTER 11.

Forced to Content

Brummell and I had often visited Brighton together in the past. As it happened, I had even taken him to his first brothel there, when he was still a Cornet in my regiment. After my health was back, and I was able to enjoy myself about the town once again, I was surpriz'd to chance upon this very man whilst walking along the Steyne (the promenade spot of that little town.) I had been very anxious to consult with him for some long while, so this *bonne chance* was certainly no displeasure to me.

"My dear Beau," I called, addressing him by what was by then universally accepted to be his formal title, "what a happy accident to see you here!"

He smiled at me and greeted me in a friendly manner; and yet I sensed some thing a mote withdrawn about his manners. It reminded me of when he had related to me his little story of his adventure in Rutland's regiment.

"Prinny," said he, "I knew if I were to find you anyplace, it should be here." He began to make good-natured inquiries as to whether I had a horse in the races that year, how I was finding the season, *etc. etc. etc.* I answered all of it with cheer enough, for I was so glad that my friend, whose conversation I had wish'd so long to hear, was again at my side.

"I have been eager to speak with you, for some while," said I. "Did Lord Byron really have you so busy in Nottinghamshire, that you could find no time to visit me?"

"Aw, he had me dreadfully so. I planned so many dinners there was scarcely time to eat any of them, and the balls and parties were so relentless I could scarcely undress for bed before another would be underway."

"My dear Brummell, now that I have you to myself, we must not let this moment pass us by. Come! I will take you to the Pavilion for dinner this evening, with Maria and me."

"Oh, I am sorry," said Brummell, somewhat wincing. "I already have promised myself elsewhere to dine."

"Then," I suggested, "let us take a walk. We can talk here, surely?"

To this Brummell agreed, and we strolled side by side. When paired together, Brummell and I could draw every glance that was to be had from a creature possessing eyes. Nothing pleased me more than such attention; still, I had my concerns to address to him. Pride would not admit me to feel as if I begged for his help, yet I did not wish to under-represent the importance it would be to receive his input towards my condition.

"My dear Mr. Brummell," said I. "Your talent for good taste has often proved indispensable to me. I am in a position right now where I am greatly in need of your keen eye."

"When are you not?" he said automatically. There was a flash across his face, as if he recognized that he ought not to have said that, but he was too late to withdraw it, and his hope now rested in his power to own it. "My dear Prinny," said he, "I am always at your disposal, to provide assistance. Whensoever you have needed me, I have been there to help, howsoever I might."

I greatly desired his help, so I allowed it to pass. "Surely you have seen the dreadful things they are writing about me in the papers? The vile cartoons they draw of me?"

"The fact is, I have been trying to stay out of politics," answered Brummell, implying thereby that he was not too familiar with the circumstance.

"Well, if you could make a fashion of *that*, I should be grateful," I replied with sarcasm. "In the meanwhile, some thing must be done for the purpose of improving my image. If I must look upon one more 'Prince of Whales' drawing, I will positively go mad. Is there any thing you might suggest towards attracting the public eye to some more flattering view of me?"

"Aw, I suppose it is a matter of how far you are willing to go," said he.

"I shall do any thing. This torment must be put to an end," said I.

"Very well," said Brummell. "Then the first thing you must do, is to promise that you will not be cross with me, for any thing I shall tell you."

I arched my brow at that. "What sort of advice requires a promise such as that?" I said indignantly.

Brummell kept his pleasant smile, yet he now seemed discomfited, like a person forc'd to deliver bad news. "Good advice is not always kind," he said. "You must abide a trifle of insult, or some thing that might resemble such, if you would have me to answer such a tremendous question."

I was appalled. "Do you mean to say that if I wish to receive your help, I must grant *you* the permission to insult me *too?*"

He suddenly became quite deferential. "Your Royal Highness, I would not wish for you to think of it in that way…"

At that moment, up the Steyne came bounding a peculiar local character of Brighton. His name was Henry Cope, and he was well known about the town, for he had a most peculiar habit of dress: *every* thing he wore was green, shoes, stockings, cravat, all green green green. It was reported that every thing in his house was likewise green, and that he ate nothing but vegetables, for their color. Evidently, Brummell and I had attracted his gaze; and being the bold and amiable character that he was, he cheerfully approached the two of us in greeting, thereby interrupting our discourse.

"Good day to you, sirs," said he. "May I but say, you are both dress'd so splendidly!"

Brummell and I pull'd together, and we bowed and thank'd him but civilly for his compliment.

"Have we met before?" he asked. "You both seem familiar to me, as if we are acquainted."

It was very possible that in some past moment of good feeling, I might have consented to an introduction with this fellow, but certainly if so, we had not renewed the acquaintance. As I fumbled my tongue for a suitable answer, Brummell pulled upon the tasseled cord that leaked down his right front side, in order to take out his gold and silver pocket watch. He made a shew of checking the time.

"Oh, your Highness," he said, loudly enough for the green man to hear, "I really must be on my way, to meet my dinner obligations for this evening. As for the matter we have discoursed upon: call upon me when we are again in London, and I shall be glad to assist you in any way that I can."

Flustered, I could do little but bow to him and bid him a good evening. Brummell hurried away, leaving me with the curious green creature, who was by then too capable of guessing at my identity. He began to bow and practically grovel before me, whilst paying me every compliment he could conceive to be fit for a Prince. I need confess that I was too much flattered by it, in that moment, to harbour any thought to turn him away. His most agreeable compliments won him a seat by my side at the nearby Coffee-House, where I purchased the verdant fellow a drink of green tea, and relished in his eager attentions. I am, too much, susceptible to flattery of the sort he offered; and particularly at this time in my life, I felt that I required it more than ever.

CHAPTER 12.

Blunt Boar, Rough Bear, or Lion Proud

I do not know why it is that I seem to eat in quantities that enlarge my figure so vastly. I eat only till I am not hungry, just like every one else. Why does it send me spreading, when a man like Brummell, Byron, or Raikes can feed at the same rate but remain as lean and muscular as Adonis? It came, *in tandem*, that I found even my tightening belt was become inadequate to contain me. My morning act of lacing up was making itself into a vile and grotesque session of torture, as the extreme pressure of the garment was bringing me to vomit and faint at least once every day. Notwithstanding that, I absolutely refus'd to relinquish control over myself. I urged the valets to proceed, even as I leaned over a chamber-pot to puke out the excess filling which the stays squeezed up from my insides. By the conclusion of the session, I had a waist that becomingly measured fifty-five inches around. My sweat drenched face was then washed, leeched and powdered, and the remainder of my daily garments applied, as I huffed at smelling salts and vinegar to stay upright. I was not willing to give up the ghost: I would not fail in my presentation before people who would judge me by my looks. I would sooner be crush'd to death and die handsome than live to be ridiculed and disdain'd.

By the time that I return'd to London it was apparent, nevertheless, that I was outgrowing my current belt. I was reluctant to procure a new one, as that would alter my measurements and force me to give up many of my favourite costumes. My wardrobe by then was very extensive, taking up multiple rooms of my house; and the clothes were all of the utmost quality, it really would be a pity to lose any. I resolv'd to send instructions to my cook, that my meals would have to be reduced in their richness. I needed to eat like a prisoner, if my figure was to be reclaimed. For weeks, then, my life was punctuated by meager, sorry meals of boiled fish and weak broth at Carlton House.

In the meanwhile, matters seem'd to grow more dire, and more humiliating, by the day. The cartoonists were able to devise some new degradation to subject me to, in their scribblings, with as much speed as the work could be printed. I had to find some thing to quash the uproar, to stop this attack against me when I had done nothing whatsoever that should deserve it. It was not possible for me to change the government in any short amount of time, much less demonstrate the change in an appreciable manner; but I could, perhaps, mimick my Royal father's strategy, and create an impression of myself as a respectable family man, instead of as a lewd sea-monster. Alas! This might require the assistance of a real monster: Caroline. I felt like Andromeda being offered up in sacrifice, as I entered her drawing room once again, stooping to speak with her about this urgent and unpleasant state of affairs.

I found her to be dressed with an unusual amount of care and I dare say success, on this occasion. I imagined it might be for the reason that I had announced myself ahead of the visit: I thus hoped that her special attention to her *toilette* could be a favourable omen, marking that she had hopes to impress me. Afterall, if my position were raised, so might hers be.

"My dear George," she said with an utterly forc'd smile, arms widespread for an embrace. "It has been ages! Why, it must have been five years since you came to see me last."

"You know, then, that it is with very important subjects that I come now," said I. "I do not enjoy taking up your time, with unimportant affairs of mine."

"Affairs are all you are ever about, George," she said, compelling me into that embrace which she seem'd to want only for the reason that I did not. Yet, it was my purpose to ask a favour of her, so I did my utmost to remain happy and pleasant.

"It is a delight to see that you are well," I said. "How has our Charlotte been? She wrote me, to ask if she might see you for your birth-day."

"She is doing wonderfully," said Caroline. "But you see her whenever you like, and so you surely know that. So what is it that brings you here to-day? Another ill-conceived attempt to woo me back into your Royal arms?"

I wanted to snap back with an insult, but that would end the conversation I had designed before it could be undertaken at all. I kept my temper. "Do not be rude, Caroline. The fact of the matter is that I have come here to propose a change in our conditions which will be of benefit to the both of us."

"You were a bit thinner on our wedding night, George. Were I to let you mount me now, I should be burst apart by your smothering weight, my insides spraying about the room like a sausage exploding from the casing."

141

I winced in horror. It was as if she were for ever *looking* to humiliate me. This weird imagination of hers was exactly why I never did become fond of her, and her babbling was the sort of thing that would utterly degrade me, were it said in public, which her unguarded tongue was eternally apt to do. "Caroline, *please!*" I admonished. "Do not be morbid. I am not here to propose any thing of that sort. I am quite satisfied with our current arrangement, and have been for as long as I have known you." I endeavor'd to soften my tone now. "Nevertheless, this is precisely the sort of thing I came here to speak about, to-day. I would like to create a more favourable public image, for the both of us to enjoy. I am here right now to propose that we make a bit of a shew. It is my conceit that we let every body see us reunited, in a peaceful state, happy and contented. We might attend balls and dinners together, and let ourselves be seen together publicly on occasion. I do not suggest that we ought to actually share our bed again, I am suggesting merely that we put on a shew of friendship."

"A shew, a shew!" she laughed, her forced sweetness cracking away. "What am I, an actress? Why is nothing real to you, George?"

"Naturally, the less we should speak with one another, the better," said I.

"So: we put on a shew? What, then, happens a year from now? Five years? Do you really expect us to sit side by side for the rest of our lives, like properties on a stage, not talking?"

I shrank at that, for there was truth in what she said. "Surely we need not be together at all times; but for the near future it could really be of immense benefit —"

"— to you and you alone."

"You are wrong about that," I retorted. "Naturally your public image will be as well enhanced as mine, if we seem to be a Royal couple in a happy condition; and that says nothing of how it shall benefit our Charlotte, who is fast approaching a marriageable age. The suitors will flock to her — the Princes, the Kings — if she is the daughter of a Royal couple that every one in Europe can envy, during these difficult times."

"Charlotte has enough interested suitors for a girl her age. That nice Mr. Brummell introduced her to a wonderful Prussian boy in the Dragoons."

I was stunned, and even I was unsure whether the cause was more from the news that Charlotte was already being courted by some person, or if it was from knowing that Brummell had been in contact with her. I certainly had not ever introduced them. "What the devil is *Brummell's* business arranging suitors for my daughter?" I gasped aloud.

"Oh, he is the lover of her aunt Frederica. Every body knows that. They see her all the time. And it is well that they should: for the *ton* is run on his advice, not yours. I have new friends and new allies in this current climate, George; to prop your blubber up on my back, is not a prospect which appeals to me in the slightest. You will have to do better than that if you should like to see me act out a happy wife to an effeminate, Frenchified, fopling such as you."

I raised my head in disdain. I hated to bargain with her, especially when she insulted me so, but I knew there must be some thing I should be able to offer to her, that would compel her co-operation with my objectives. "Name your terms, then. Do you want money? Castles? Clothes?"

"I want to have some enjoyment of my life, George," she said with evident frustration. "That is never to happen, with a selfish *Dummkopf* such as you for ever about. Sorry, my dear, but there is no accord. I have plans already laid, which are not to involve you."

"Plans? For what?" I asked with skepticism.

"For a new life, free from you, free from your oppression, free to be free." She smiled, and extended her arms to shew off her delightful garments. "How do you like this dress, George? I had an entire new wardrobe made this year. Mr. Brummell approved every design. I am expecting to live out the high life, George, without you."

Now I was turned from perturb'd to worried. She realized, it seemed, that I needed her more than she did me, and she was not going to grant me any of her lofty favours. It annoyed me, and I began to grow angry. I decided to revise my tactic: if I could not *give* her any thing that would motivate, perhaps I could *deprive* her of some thing. "I will have your allowance revoked, and see you rot away in some crumbling country manor."

"You have not the authority to do either of those things," said Caroline, quite coldly. "That is up to Parliament, and I think they will not bear the shame of letting the Princess of Wales live in poverty. And this property is my own, you cannot remove me from it."

She was correct. It enraged me all the more. "D--- you, Caroline, stop being such a b---h and co-operate with me! Surely you expected to have some kind of duty to perform, when you married me. Your life cannot be all drinking and concealing your lovers."

"I know you like to keep yours openly," she said. "But I have done my duty: I made Charlotte. Now go away, George, if this is all you are here about. I am not going to gratify your desires."

I could feel myself quake with outrage. "It is not for you to refuse me, over a matter such as this! So help me, I will destroy you: I will tell every one that you were not a virgin on our wedding night."

She rolled her eyes at me. Can you believe it? *Rolled* her *eyes*! "George, if that is the whole of your attack, I

145

advise you not to bother. You were in a treasonous marriage to a Catholic, on our wedding night. You fornicate with whores and actresses. You obsess over a young man and his tight clothes. In short, you should not sew thorns when you are walking barefoot, yourself."

My hold over my temper was lost at that. I let out a scream of frustration, and I commend myself for not having done some undignified thing like to overturn furniture or throw vases. "You," I said in answer to her accusation, "are the one always *obsessed* with Mr. Brummell! Why, you bring up his name every d----d time I stoop to visit with you!"

"Did I *say* Brummell?" she asked with a smile.

"What other person could you mean? You always start on the subject of Brummell, Brummell, Brummell! And you wonder why I obsess over him? I obsess over him only because every one in this whole city is obsessed with him! They all act as if he is some kind of King! You know what? Very well. Do not give me any help! You despise me too greatly: no matter. I will just *kill myself*, right now, and you shall be *entirely* done with me! I will jump from your top floor window, and be smashed all over your garden! Every one will blame you for my murder, you regicidal German whore!"

"For the love of Heaven, George, perhaps Mrs. Fitzherbert will bear this conduct from you, but not I!" She

146

stood up and rang the bell for the servants while I began for the stairs to carry out my threat. By Heaven, it would have been worth it to me to die then, just to humiliate her; but in an instant, her servants were sprung into the room, and she instructed them to take hold of me and haul me out. I fought: it required the combined forces of several footmen to subdue me and force me to the door. She scream'd at me, not at all concerned that these men might do me some injury:

"It is shameful how you comport yourself! You know what Brummell said to me, the last time I saw him?" I was hurried out of the room, I still thrashing and striving futilely to grab walls and furniture so I would not be put out. "He said — this is exactly what he said — he said, 'Pay no mind to Prinny. I made him what he is, and I can unmake him.' He is right, you know. You may be destin'd to be King, but so was Louis in France: and you know what his lack of popularity did to him!"

When I was hauled into the hallway I demanded to be released, and my wish was granted, though I remained well supervised as I shewed myself to the front door to make exit from this unholy Bedlam. I return'd from there to Carlton House, and when I arrived home, I call'd at once for brandy, cakes and cheese. Thus ended my regimen of meager foods. Thus ended, too, on that day, my hope for self-improvement of any sort.

CHAPTER 13.

Twenty Thousand Tongues

I learnt the identity of Charlotte's paramour and immediately had his regiment sent away to Spain. Every body disapproved of this action: my own mother the Queen, Charlotte's namesake, wrote me a reprimand for it, admonishing me for being too strict with my daughter. I, too strict! Do you suppose I ever got to choose my own spouse? No, I had to sneak behind every body's back just to woo my dear Maria, whose affection even now I held only most tenuously, thanks to the endeavors of every one around me to destroy the match I longed for. Notwithstanding whatever might happen in the future, Charlotte was daughter of a King, and deserved a better spouse than some soldier picked out for her by a well-dressed rake. She was not even old enough to be "out" yet, but then that brings me to a new complaint: —

To be presented at Court had long been the ritual that marked the turning point in an aspirant society girl's life. Once presented, in the Presence Chamber at St. James, she was "out." She was available to marry, and by having been seen at the Court, she was regarded as a worthy wife and friend to all of the *haute ton*. Past errors were wiped from memory, and her happy road to public life could begin.

Yet the word, relay'd to me by the Corinthians, was that this major ritual was coming to be seen as an unnecessary formality; for what really matter'd to a girl's public reception, was whether or not *Mr. Brummell approved of her.*

Yes, that cynical creature continu'd to elevate himself in the public eye. He had been invited (*invited!!!*) to an honorary position at the exclusive assembly rooms at Almack's, alongside the Lady Patronesses. There was no better assembly room than Almack's; peers were sometimes excluded as unworthy to dance there. It was run by a council of fashionable women, amongst them the current Lady Jersey, who was daughter-in-law of my old mistress Frances. Evidently, she had come to greatly favour Brummell after the "Mistress Fitzherbert" slight had so pleased her mother-in-law. Now he was made an honorary member of that sacred council, governing the most important ballroom in all of England. He assisted in the decisions as to what person was worthy to be permitted the honor of buying a ticket, or in determining whether some existing member had fallen too far afoul of good taste and must be excluded from future dances. It all was up to his whims; one of my Corinthians was dismissed from the club on the pretext that Brummell did not believe him to be an adequately graceful dancer. That was all that it took to be cut from the holy guest-list of Almack's.

Brummell's clout, and his luck at the card tables, had provided him with access to funds enough to change his place of residence from Chesterfield Street to a just slightly larger abode at the nevertheless much more fashionable address of Chapel Street, which property I later learnt was furnish'd to him by the generosity of the Duke of Gloucester. His visitors still choked the road every morning, but every body was glad to have access to the Beau and to be present in his regard.

And still he made so splendid a shew and display of his devotion to me: such a spectacle that it would have been a humiliation to *me* were I to cut him socially. Why, were I to have gone forward with it, I should seem like some selfish monster who did not treasure even his dearest friends and most loyal supporters! Brummell carried an umbrella with an ivory portrait of me carved into the handle. He kept expensive snuff-boxes with my image upon them. He made it known to every body that he was a loyal supporter of his dear friend Prinny. I must suppose that the magical influence which this association held over the debt collectors was not without sway over his loyalty to me. Notwithstanding this, the politically charged atmosphere about the city was becoming a disturbance to him. He was a member of the gentleman's club at White's: a place with strong Tory leanings. Most of my supporters favoured the Whig-friendly rival club of Brooks's. (Though I dare say neither party seem'd to be very pleased with me of late.) This was creating some awkwardness for the Beau at his place of business, for it was at White's that he customarily exercised his skill with cards, or tried his luck at other wagers. There was talk, along with his friends Mildmay, Alvanley and Pierrepoint, that Brummell should open his own gentleman's club.

"One without political affiliations," said Pierrepoint. "No talk of serious matters at all: nothing but leisure, beauty and sport, as it well ought to be."

"My duties at Almack's," said Brummell, reluctantly agreeing, "have educated me about the necessities for the operation of such an enterprise."

"Then it is the most opportune moment that could ever be," said Alvanley. "The town is in dire need of such a club for people of fashion, and you have the knowledge of how to make it happen."

"We can go into it together," suggested Mildmay. "What do you say, gentlemen?"

"I think we shall need to win a little more at cards to get such an endeavor underway," said Brummell, with a blush.

"Do not worry about the money, we will see it through," said Alvanley. "For Heaven's sake, if we can merely find a better cook than Almack's, we shall be sure to succeed."

"Aw, Byron knows the best French chefs. I will ask him for advice," said Brummell.

And such was the genesis of Watier's, the ultimate place for London's gentlemen of fashion. The club was a runaway success from the moment that it opened: it had the best food in the city, and Beau Brummell was its President. It was difficult to find a person that did not wish to be a member of the club; yet Brummell, tho' he enjoyed himself there immeasurably, did not derive any income from it, as it had been his friends that had invested all the money, and thus took all the profits. His income continued to rely wholly upon Fortune's favour at the card table, supplemented by whatever he could glean from his wealthy friends and his lady *protectrices*.

He told me all of this, one afternoon at Carlton House. I had just receiv'd a large order of new shoes, which Brummell had been charged with overseeing. I might not trust his character, but I still trusted his eye. There was, at this time, a minor alteration in the shape of fashionable shoes, being a small squaring-off of the point of the toe. My collection of footwear had to be replaced with the new mode: Hessian boots, dance slippers, *et caetera*. Brummell, clean scrubbed and neatly garb'd as ever, hair arranged in the newest mode, monitored the unpacking of each pair from its private box, and I tried each one for fit and comfort. Many were new, stiff, and dreadfully galling to my feet.

"Seems like such a waste to ask my footmen to wear them in," said I.

"I never allow my shoes to be worn in," said Brummell. "It wrinkles the leather."

"A wrinkle makes a better sight than stains of blood," said I. "But then I suppose you are so idle that you never walk in your shoes to begin with."

"Aw, I would not dream of it. It would ruin the polish on the bottoms," he joked. Yet this was but half a joke: the man really did get the soles of his shoes blackened, just as he did the tops. The pair which he wore at this moment were as shiny and spotless as the ones which were being drawn freshly from their boxes.

"Is that the reason why you never dance?" asked I.

"There is rarely a fine enough dancer available to tempt me," he replied. "If I am to shuffle badly, I would rather it be at the card table."

"I should think you would find women positively throwing themselves at you. Ever danced with Frederica?" I asked, tossing out a matter that had been fretting the back of my mind for all too long by this point. "She does quite well at it."

Brummell smiled out from his pure white collar and cravat. He was not evidently ashamed at knowing what information I knew, but he understood that he had been caught at some thing he ought not have done. "We keep it rather more discreet than all of that," said he. "Afterall, she is a married woman. To your brother."

"How in this world did you ever manage to meet her?" I asked, truly confounded by the question.

"At your wedding," answered he, then added: "The real wedding, not the Catholic one."

"Naturally," said I, "Frederica had never yet been to England when I married Maria, and you, I think, were but five years old."

"And Maria was, what, fifty at the time?"

I frowned at him. "She was nine and twenty. She is only six years older than myself... and she is not *Maria* to you, if you please."

"Mistress Fitzherbert, of course," said he with a smile.

"You know, I can stomach that malefic tongue of yours when it's directed at me, but I hate it when you point that thing at my wife," I said with gravity. "It is ungentlemanly to insult a woman, like that."

I had addressed him very calmly and respectfully, I thought, and I expected from him a reply of a similar tone.

"It's no insult to speak truth," said he. "Caroline is your real wife."

I felt slighted. "Caroline is a filthy-minded old witch whom I was forc'd to wed for financial reasons. That sacrifice pays for all of this. It pays for my little gifts to you, as well," I said pointedly, hoping to remind him of his place.

"You might not wish to boast of that," said Brummell. "There is a word for women who do such things, in the name of money, and I do not believe you should be glad were it applied upon you. Besides that, why be ashamed of Caroline? She is a more sensible woman than you think. She will not abide your falsehoods and pretense: it might be some value to you, to regard her."

I was now taking up an especially large box, which contained a pair of long boots (over the knee) which I had ordered after having seen a similar pair in an antique print, and formed a desire to have for myself. "She thinks I am trash whilst she is trash herself," I answered to Brummell, my blood heating. "And it ill becomes your famously fine taste to so respect her views."

"Forgive me," said Brummell in a tone that was not at all that of a penitent. "I only mention it, for she is better liked about the town than yourself, at this time."

I felt as if he had just slapped me across the face. "The town! The town, what matters the town? Like a lot of ungrateful children, they try to flock out on their own and decide their tastes, without yet being possessed of the wisdom to know what is good or what is right. 'She is preferred by the town.' You disgust me, Brummell."

Despite our argument, I sought to continue my task of trying shoes. I put on one of the thigh-high-up boots. Brummell groaned with dismay as he saw me.

"Good Lord, you sneak'd that order past me, did you?" said he. He was looking at me with eyes that screeched disapproval. I glared back at him defiantly, and pulled the second boot over my leg. Standing, I displayed my leather-covered limbs, which I felt made me look very fine and intimidating.

"She told me what you said about me, you know," I said to him. "'You *made me what I am*?' I should have left you to wave flags all your life as a Cornet in the Hussars."

"Well, I definitely did not make you wear *those* hideous things," he answered, as if affronted.

I could take no more. I threw my head back and pointed to the door. "You have insulted me, you have insulted my wife, and now, Mr. Brummell, you have insulted my shoes, and that, sir, is going quite too far, for nobody listens to you except for the reason that *I* had once listen'd to you. Get out!"

Recognizing that he had now violated some thing far too sacrosanct, he ask'd to excuse himself, grasping at the pretense that he left of his own choice; and for his sake I made a shew of dismissing him most gladly.

***

It was not long after this that my Regency was approved and formally enacted. From that moment onward I was the Monarch of the country for all practical purposes. It was a dream that so many in this world might have sacrificed their first-born to experience; yet I was not delighted by my new circumstance, and in fact I seem'd to require more diversion than ever to escape from the anxieties of my situation. I began to enjoy the pleasures of the dinner table with more alacrity; this, unhappily, made a greater impact upon my figure than I should have guessed. I was oblig'd at long last to put in an order for a larger model of tightening-belt. My neck-brace, too, had to be enlarged, for I was being choked by its pressure at every

157

moment. I began to suffer from severe gout, and could scarcely sleep a wink for it. And worse, there were questions being raised again about Mrs. Fitzherbert: our relationship was known in *society*, but not to the common *public*, who would never understand the complexity of my situation. I was oblig'd to have a memoir published in which I asserted that Mrs. Fitzherbert and I were *not* married and that the very conceit of such a thing was only slander sprung up from malicious gossip that had begun during a bout of anti-Catholic hysteria, started by someone who was dead now. You can imagine neither of us was pleased at that: that I was forc'd to deny her place in my life, to suggest that all the nights we had spent in the other's bed were merely between me and *some woman*. She could scarcely bear to speak to me, she was so affronted; yet in tears I begged her forgiveness and excuse, as it had been a necessity committed only to protect her from even worse investigation and slander. By God, did she not understand how I loved her? My own Maria, for whom I would die? Yet she declared that the situation was too great a distress to her, and she design'd to return to her home in Brighton for the time being. The lonely consolation of my drawing room was made my sole comfort; there I could sit and drink my favourite brandies by the fire, and admire my personal collection of prints and drawings. My health lent me an excuse to defer most political duties to my Ministers, and I was thus enabl'd to smooth those troubled waters in which I was washed, down to a level which I could nearly manage and tolerate. My great torment through all of it, though, was the question of why I was so violently disliked by every body? Had I done any thing so different from what others around me enacted every day, they without being faulted for it?

Yet I did maintain possession of a little love. My most recently acquired mistress was Isabella, the Marchioness of Hertford, who was four years my senior: and I was nearly fifty at this time, making her nothing near a youthful flower. Even I sometimes wondered at what was wrong with me, in my choice of concubines. I was addicted to beauty, so why did I always find myself with ladies that the world would see as *past their prime*? Somehow I was always most comfortable with women a little older than myself. I liked the way that they made me feel young and attractive, because, in comparison, I was.

Every day I would visit Isabella, in the afternoon, at her house in Manchester Square. My carriage was purple and yellow, a very noticeable and recognizable sight. It was always usual that people on the street would pause and stare at my equipage, but lately they had taken to do more: they would hoot and jeer at me as I passed along. I kept my curtains drawn and passed in dismay, till I could alight and find myself again in the comforting arms of my elderly mistress, where I could know just a short while's solace.

Such solace grew continuously more needful by the day, for my nights were increasingly sleepless: the gout was a constant agony to me. Even the weight of my bedsheets, grazing across my foot, were enough to send my nerves all aflame in pure misery. Several glasses of brandy and a julep of laudanum could get me well enough to sleep again, provided I did not object to sleeping through most of the following day as well. In my teens, I recall my Royal father once having stepped into my bedchamber to admonish me for staying in bed to such a late hour; to which I replied: "I find, sir, that however late I rise, the day is always quite long enough for doing nothing." Ah, those days! No longer could I laze about and do nothing: I always had correspondence to answer, Ministers to speak with, and all the other mindless tasks of political life. It exhausted me so; and in combination with my sleeplessness it was driving me nearly out of my mind. I was quite agitated all of the time; and always, in consequence, I longed for some relief and happiness.

The next time that I met, at the theatre, with my dear friends the Corinthians, we discussed the present state of affairs. We also had a new member in our ranks: somehow I had been moved to admit Mr. Cope, the green man of Brighton, to our cenacle. After all, he did have a taste of a sort; and I liked people who had a bit of folly and peculiarity about them. I also admired that he was *not* a follower of Brummell's.

We discussed the current reports of me that were blackening all the pages of the newspapers. Why was it that when Brummell lived beyond his means he was cheered and beloved as a man of style, whereas I was called a greedy and irresponsible hedonist? What secret, to win the love of the people, had he discovered, which I was missing by nature? Fox's near-toothless mouth laughed when I expressed concern at my depictions by the cartoonists. He had followed my example of donning a tightening-belt to beautify his figure, but it caused him to gesticulate strangely, rather like a marionette.

"Jealousy is all that it is," said he. "Nobody really hates, but out of jealousy."

"Do not pay it any mind, sir: ignore what they say. You do right by yourself," said Chatham, dressed in a somewhat rumpled silk suit.

"They laugh at you for your weight, because there is nothing else the matter with you," said His Kleine Excellence Tyrwhitte, whom I nicknamed The Twenty-Third of June because he is THE SHORTEST KNIGHT (ha! ha!)

But alas! I could almost be comforted by their words, except that I was becoming aware of how far the

Corinthians had fallen behind to the fashions: meaning, behind to Brummell's example. Really, behind *any* example. Here they were, overdecorated in untidy linens, stiff with whalebone, all reeking of their own chosen perfumeries, the scents of which mingled to make our box seat smell some thing reminiscent of a chemist's laboratory. And then there was that real Captain-Queernabs all in green. I just wanted to weep. These were my supporters? These were the ones who still believed in me? I looked at the boxes around us, which seem'd to me like they were full of happy, young people of fashion, all in the bloom of youth; meanwhile here was I, old, fat, gouty; and clearly was surrounded by a lot of crack-heads and rum dukes. How could I ever expect to be admired and approbated with such company, such vulgar society?

After the play, I was expected to go with the Corinthians about the town for the traditional after-theatre anonymous fornication with prostitutes, but I excused myself from their company, citing that I felt too unwell. Indeed, my gout was irritating me, though a little more brandy was all that would have been necessary to quash that. In truth, I merely wished to be alone.

I remembered myself in my prime, back in the seventeen-hundred-and-eighties, when I was considered a dashing fellow, and I set all the fashions. We wore floral hues back then, can you believe it? And continual clouds of white powder about our shoulders. Gentlemen would lounge about all day in their nightcaps and dressing gowns, receiving visitors in this condition, burning scented pastilles to purify the air from any stink. How I missed those times. To be beloved by those one does not love back is no flattery, it is like an insult that such trash is all that finds you fond and lovable. Even Adonis, when chased by the goddess Venus herself, saw no happiness in it, for he did not love her back or even like her. How hateful it is to be loved by that which repulses one's senses! And how awful it is, when one is left to be that same shameful creature which repels that very thing which one loves! To love, to strive to win another's love, and find one's most earnest efforts met only with rejection and embarrassment is one of the worst tortures that can be put upon a human soul. We were made to love: not merely as men and women, but as brothers, friends and countrymen, yet we find these connexions grows more and more scarce as we age. What is it that kills the love in us, and deprives us of it? Alas! These are questions for the philosophers. I shall grant some patronage to a few, and ask them to determine this answer for me.

CHAPTER 14.

Foolish-Witty

What was this addiction to the Beau George Brummell which I harboured? In spite of all my internalized resentment for him, still I went to visit him regularly. His parlor was a veritable *saloon* of all the men of fashion: "dandies" as they were coming to be known. They followed Brummell's example and embraced beauty at the expense of all else — of manners, sense, utility; all were out the window to make room for what was pleasing to the eye alone. I had no wish or desire to be the recipient of his rebukes and insults, yet to lack his attention and notice at all, was a feeling that was still worse than his greatest affronts.

Conducted by a servant, I made my way through the tumult of tradesmen who were decorating the halls, each one waiting to speak with Brummell about his unpaid bills. I proceeded to the drawing room directly. Before I could enter, I could perceive the words of conversation which then took place inside, and I marked that my name was being spoken. I could recognize the Scottish lilt of Lord Fyfe's speech to say: "...which Prinny should undertake." I slowed the manservant in his progress, for I wish'd to learn what was now being said, before I would enter.

"Aw, well, it would not seem to me that Prinny's been missing any dinners," said Brummell. "Nor Mrs. Fitzherbert, who I think has lately been a rather bad influence upon him. I have taken to calling them Big Ben and Benina, after that ill-tempered pugilist." He referred here to Benjamin Brain, the prize-fighter, who was famous for his feuds. "For the both of them seem to have nothing but frowns, contentions and bad humor about them, of late."

"You say he is strong?" asked Fyfe.

"No, I say he is *Big*," answered Brummell, who gained a laugh from this. "But she is bigger. I would have to widen the very room to ever have her over. Why, I doubt if she can find a set of whalebone stays, since she is bigger than a whale."

My heart exploded with fury. I myself could stomach the degradation of Brummell's insults, but my Maria — never! I entered the room at that moment, and was announced by the servant. The beaux shewed no shame for how they had been talking; but that was natural, for it was part of the *maniere de faire* to suffer these sorts of insults, within their circle. The expectation seemed to be that it was all in good fun and nobody should take it badly, no matter how much affronted one should be. To insult my beloved wife, the most beautiful creature I had ever known — that was another matter. My spirit raced with wrath and hatred for that, though the physical body remained settled.

"And here is the *great* man himself," said Brummell, rising to greet me.

I was less pleas'd to greet him that I might have been, but I bore it with (I think) grace. I was acquainted with most of the crowd: the spendthrift Hungarian prince Esterhazy, and Lords Cholmondeley, Fyfe, Wilton, Alvanley and Yarmouth. The drawing room at this house was decorated extensively with mirrors, and I could see my reflection in several. It was disheartening, how old and fat I looked when compared against these *gens qui marquent être quelque chose*. I could see my face powder was caking in the creases upon my skin, and I took up my handkerchief: with pretense of blotting at sweat I made efforts to smooth the composition back into place.

Wilton addressed me, looking for me to provide him with some information in regards to the latest scandal: "Is it true what they say of the Princess of Wales?"

"You mean Caroline?" I asked. "What is it that they say of her?"

"That she's taken a lover and means to go away with him to the continent."

This was news to me; but then it was not really any of my business. "I speak but little with Caroline; and though she speaks freely when she speaks to me, we have had no reason to discuss this matter."

Wilton seemed disappointed that I had nothing salacious to contribute to the report. Not long after this, a young man, pudgy and awkward in figure, was ushered into the room by Brummell's valet; he was a young aspirant, evidently known to Brummell but not yet to the rest of us. We offered our greetings to him, but we were not introduced. The poor young creature was put in a seat among us. He was obviously dressed in his best clothing, and by his manners and costume was certainly to be supposed the son of a good, even noble family; but it all amounted to a sorry attempt at fashionability in the midst of this exalted crowd. Several of the men began to stare at him aggressively, taking up their spyglasses to examine him. He was like the jay in the fable, looking to blend in with the peacocks; and he was about to be plucked bald.

"My dear fellow," said Brummell. "Aw, where did you pick up that extraordinary affair you have upon your back?"

"Maybe it's an heirloom?" suggested Fyfe.

"It is coeval with Alfred the Great," said Alvanley, "at least."

The young man was coloring with humiliation. "Is there some thing the matter with my coat?" he asked.

"Coat!" exclaimed Brummell.

"Coat!" echoed the chorus of his friends.

"That is no more like a coat than a cauliflower: if it is, I will be d----d," said Brummell.

The young man was flustered and it was plain that he had no notion of how to respond to this unbenevolent criticism. It was evident to me that his invitation into the group had been intended for a test of his commitment to dandyism. Clearly he was a failure in this: a real dandy would have known how to bear this friction, either by sparring verbally or else by suffering it contentedly. The unhappy youth merely waited out a polite fifteen minutes, then excused himself from the party with a face reddened by shame. Nobody was sorry to see his departure.

Back at ease with only the regular society, Brummell unleashed a snuff box from his pocket. A few of us followed him in suit: I have explained before, this ritual was enacted less in the name of the snuff, than to make a display of our magnificent boxes and jewelry. Nobody in this room held a snuff box to be ashamed for, and therefore we all complemented one another for the taste and workmanship infused in each man's little prize. Of course,

Brummell had the best of them: it was that darling darling darling little turtle box which he would carry from time to time. It had been an object of my utmost admiration for many years.

"Truly a lovely specimen," said Alvanley of it.

"Indeed," said I. "Tell me: is it one you might be willing to part with?"

Brummell was intrigued by this proposition. "Do you mean to buy it from me?"

"To buy it, or to make an exchange for it." I held out my hands and he allowed me to touch the box. "I have been eyeing it for ages. I even endeavour'd to have an identical one made by the jeweler, but they botch'd up the face so badly that it better resembled a drowned cat: I had it melted down for a toothbrush, *enfin*."

"For your sake, I might be willing to part with this one," said Brummell. "Do you have one to exchange for it? I would not wish to be minus one of my treasury."

"What if, say, I take this box for myself; and you may go to Gray's, the jewelers, and pick out any replacement you like?"

Brummell seemed pleased by this proposal. "Might I have one made to order?"

"If you wish it," said I.

The deal was agreed to, in the presence of the city beaux: I pocketed the adorable little turtle, and left

Brummell to place his order at Gray's. But I had a scheme up my sleeve against that two-faced little Gemini: I waited about a week and a half, to be sure that the order had been placed; at which point I conveyed to Gray my wish that the order be cancelled. I told him that I would inform Brummell of the situation myself. But of course, I said nothing of the matter whatsoever to Brummell, and merely waited for him to discover the facts in his own time.

After this, I made an invitation for Brummell to attend the theatre with me. He agreed. We watched a well-known play with the finest actors, at which, as usual, Brummell's mere presence was the main attraction to all the crowd; and when we went to meet the actors in the Green Room after the shew, they all flock'd to *him*, whilst he was cold and unimpress'd to see the greatest names of the London stage. After the theatre, we undertook the traditional stay with some *abbesses of Covent Garden*, to use the learned term. I directed him to a particular establishment with which I was familiar.

"The women at this one are incomparable," said I. I drew him in; it was a fine enough house in its look, and the women were pretty enough. We were brought more liquor, and an assortment of eager strumpets surrounded us, each endeavoring to attract our attentions. In time we each made a choice of one, and took them away to private chambers.

I spent the evening with mine, but I did not indulge myself with her as one might have expected. I limited myself to some frivolous conversation and the receiving of a few kisses. I was not about to stick my p---- in any of *those* women; for it had been warn'd to me that every girl at that place had the French Disease, and had been docked for it. However, I made no mention of this fact to Brummell. Gentlemen did not discuss these diseases with one another, afterall; even if we might talk of the women who provided them. It was like a curse which, to speak of, might inflict itself upon you. Yet after that night, Brummell did not have to speak of it: in time, his morning levées and public washing rituals were making it all too apparent that some unfortunate thing had happened to him. A rash form'd upon his hands and feet: he began to wear his gloves everywhere and anywhere, to disguise this from the public. Soon thereafter, he developed a fever. One of his visitors, remarking that he seem'd unwell, receiv'd a characteristick reply: "I have caught a cold," said he. "But what could I expect? I was put into bed with a damp s-----." Soon after this, he required a temporary stay upon his visitors, for he was too painfully ill to see any body. When I heard of this, I sent him a letter wishing him to get well soon: and then, I hurried out with invitations and in putting my own servants to work, for I threw a ball or a grand dinner party nearly every night, my reason being that with Brummell out of service, I was the city's main attraction. Every one came to Prinny for their entertainment. Every one came to Prinny for advice. Princes were envied. And for a little while it seemed to me, as if perhaps all could be well; perhaps I was not so badly viewed as I had dreaded. People came to me! People delighted in visiting me! It was like old times again, back when I was fresh and full of life.

Of course the doctors all about the town were familiar with French Disease, and knew how to treat it: some, it was said, even knew how to cure it. Naturally Mr. Brummell did not advertise his treatments any more than he did his disease, but in time he got better; at least well enough to resume his normal "duties" about the town. The Chapel Street levées resumed, Almack's reapplied its most rigid standards of beauty, and my poor house was left empty again.

After Mr. Brummell's recuperation, he wrote to me a friendly note, in which he mark'd his discovery that the order for the snuff box at Gray's, which I had promis'd to him, seem'd to have been cancelled. The note that he wrote me was d---ably polite; he supposed there had been some mistake, or a need for me to change my plans. He did not fault me for it; the one request which he did make, nevertheless, was that I might be good enough to return the snuff box which I had taken from him, for it was given upon the promise that I would supply him a new one. I simply ignored his letter. I had, without ceremony, cut the syphilitic son of a b---h from my society, and saw no need to reply to it. I had invoked his own tricks, his false friendship and cruel underhandedness, to bring him to the ruin he deserved. I was done with him: I had bested him at last. I was no longer going to abide his insults against me, against my wife, or his interference with all the most sacred structures of society. The wretch thought that he was not under the power of the Prince; well, I had proved him wrong.

For all the misfortune upon him, Lady Luck seem'd to have favoured him at cards in some sort of effort to compensate. He had lately won an almost unheard of £20,000 at the table. To commemorate this achievement, he and his core dandy friends were to throw an extravagant ball: one which I daresay must have consumed a goodly portion of the funds it was meant to celebrate having gained. Every body who was any body in the *ton* was to be there. Frances, Isabella, even Caroline were invited (though I understood the lattermost to have left the country for Italy by then, praise be to God.) Lord Byron would be there. Frederica and my brother were to attend. Not a name was missing from the guest list, but for one. It was mine. This was surely no oversight: the Beau must have known I had cut him, and have therefore influenced his friends (with whom I was still connected) not to invite me as any guest of their own. And yet, as Prince Regent, I did not need an invitation. It was like a modern *droit du seigneur*: if I chose to attend at any ball or assembly, invited or not, it was considered an honor to the hosts to have me there. Naturally Mr. Brummell was to be at this event, and I surely had no desire to see him again; but I took into consideration how many others whom I dearly loved and wish'd to see, would be there. Was that wretch to deprive me of my company, of my happiness? Never! I wrote to the hosts of this party, announcing my plans to attend notwithstanding their little oversight about inviting me. There was no need to ask their *permission*.

The fashionable Argyle Rooms had been rented to accommodate this glorious event. It is a most splendid location: the entrance hall is painted with frescos of Corinthian pilasters and compartments, footed with green marble. It was there, waiting to greet the guests, that I saw my four hosts in all their tasteful finery: Alvanley, Mildmay, Pierrepoint and, naturally, the Beau himself. They were lined up, two to each side, in suits so well tailored that there was not a single wrinkle between them.

It was my polite duty to greet them. I began at the left side, speaking first to Mildmay; then across to Pierrepoint. Beside him was Brummell, eyes glaring at me despite his false smile. I passed him over, making every display of not having noticed him at all, as if the man were no more visible to me than a f--t. People around us saw what I had done; I could feel a sudden chill to course through the whole room. I had just affronted the great Beau Brummell, and made known to every body my cut of his company. I crossed back to the left to greet Alvanley, and that done, was about to make my way up to the vestibule and stairs.

Then loudly, loudly, oh! so loud, there was a cry from behind my shoulder in the voice which I knew belong'd to Brummell:

"Aw, Alvanley, *who is your fat friend?*"

Every person who stood in that passageway cringed. There was a moment of silence as nobody knew what to do. Then I heard, dreadfully, the rising sound of a giggle: a crescendo that soon became a mighty roar of laughter. Every body was laughing; and this delight was being had at my expense. Brummell was plainly quite pleased with himself to have thus humiliated me.

I refus'd to let myself be beaten back, and I went forward in a vain effort to enjoy the party; my collar kept my head held high; but my bitterness at the affront, and the whispers and stares I receiv'd as news of my humiliation was dispersed amongst the merrymakers, dampened my spirits too much to remain. I took an early leave, and retired alone to the quiet darkness of Carlton House, to my cherry brandy, to my laudanum juleps.

The mark of a great party comes of certain elements: that every body have a gay time, that there be a spectacle, and that every body come out with a story to tell. I became the story of that night: every one talked of how Beau Brummell had cut the Prince Regent with such a brilliantly simple insult. Always simple and refined in his tastes, that Brummell.

CHAPTER 15.

Blessed Bankrupt

I took it upon myself to send word to every bank and creditor I knew of in London, to very dutifully and politely inform them that Mr. Brummell was no longer under my protection. The news that he had lost my patronage and friendship spread swiftly enough through that sphere of society. Soon the front lobby at Watier's was compacted with moneylenders and tradesmen who waited for him to emerge from his nightly games, that they could demand he repay them without further delay. Before, had they taken him to Court for his debt, there was an assumption that I might have stepped in to interfere: and perhaps they were right to presume as much. Now, without me, he was fair game to for the hunters. It was the custom in those days that gentlemen's debts went unpaid for years, but Brummell had stretch'd all his grace periods past the limit, and the lenders had no more reason to grant him leniency.

The Beau began to frequent White's club once again, with more regularity, I should even say preference, than ever before. Perhaps it was his hope to make new friends in politics. I do not have any impression that such a venture was any profit to his income, though he perhaps did gain a few more cheerful men of his acquaintance, who would fawn over him and pay him compliments for his appearance whilst accepting his insults to theirs.

In an effort to acquire the funds he needed to repay his debts, he began to gamble harder at the tables: but his forlorn hopes were met with disappointment more often than not. The gifts of his friends, of course, assured that his actual lifestyle was not too much altered, but the ready capital he needed if he was to put an end to his old debts was for ever eluding him. His morning levées were being interrupted with visits from men who would come presenting bills which they asserted could not be anymore delayed for repayment. He began to borrow from friends, with promises to return the money at some future time; but his luck never changed for the better, and he found himself unable to keep these promises.

After this went on with an exceptional patience from all sides, a fellow member at White's, Richard Meyler, hereafter known as "Dick the Dandy-Killer" demanded repayment for some £7,000 he had provided to Brummell. The penniless Beau was unable to offer any thing that could appease his unhappy creditor-friend. Under the direction of this gentleman, Brummell was presented at last with a summons for the Debtor's Court: a debt which he knew already he could not repay — yet he had to repay it, or he should find himself imprisoned in the squalor of the Marshalsea or the Fleet for his failure to comply.

The next morning, the Beau's toiletries, clothes and some keepsakes were missing from his house; his curricle and horses were gone, as was Brummell himself. He had been observed at the Opera the night before, but no person was knowledgable of his whereabouts after that. It was as if he had simply disappeared, like an outdated fashion. He was never seen in London again, and his residence, situation and circumstance were unknown.

Mr. Christie, the auctioneer, sold off what was left inside the Beau's Chapel Street house, the proceeds going to reimburse the former creditors. There was great interest in the sale, and many of the *ton*, the dandies, the Etonians and his other old friends came to purchase keepsakes that had been abandoned by the *best figure in England*. His large collection of snuff-boxes was of an especial interest. There was one blue and buff box, set with small gemstones, in which was found a note reading: "This snuff-box was intended for the Prince Regent, if he had conducted himself with more propriety towards me." The utter nerve! "Had I conducted myself with more propriety towards him?" And he made a point of labeling the box with this!

Needless to say, the box was sold to an unknown high bidder. It now sits in my case, with the other I took from him. His furniture, casks of wine, library and art collection all were sold off, in their turns. Bits of his memory litter the curiosity cabinets of all the finest men and women in the city. Brummell is gone; only his legend remains.

CHAPTER 16.

Their Course to Paphos

Why, alas! am I not better looking? Why could I not be but one-third better looking than I was made to be? I am not ugly: some have even called me a handsome gentleman. Yet I have never been envied for my looks. Surely, would I have been I only a few degrees finer in my appearance, all my life would be better. I would not have been made to suffer the hapless misfortunes which I have encountered, had I been possessed of the greater respect and awesomeness that a finer face, figure and complexion could have provided unto me.

It had been my business for some while to fix the marriage of my daughter, Charlotte. She was at this time aged around nineteen years, and never a prettier girl of that age had lived. I had been endeavoring to arrange for her to marry someone who became her, someone with a suitable status to make the husband of a someday-King's daughter, if God should will me to live so long to reach that exalted station. For Charlotte, I had set my sights upon the Prince of Orange, who was heir apparent to the Netherlands; our negotiations for the union were already long underway, and to my mind were practically fix'd. He came to England, and when I receiv'd him, I certainly did not neglect to introduce Charlotte to him. She was courteous and well-manner'd, and yet, it would appear, she was less than favourably impress'd by her intended. I was disappointed at this turn, but I continued with my plans for her despite it, for I felt myself confident that the situation would not be altogether disagreeable to her. Afterall, it was not as the case was with her mother and I, in which my mistress Frances had influenced the match and deliberately chose for me a spouse she knew I could never be pleased by. William, the Prince of Orange, seemed a suitable age, appropriate rank and a reasonable character for her: and I could see no other matrimonial alliance so desirable as this one. Charlotte, certainly, would not despise him.

Then my plans were all thrown out the window, when Charlotte announced to me one afternoon, accompanied by her Royal grandmother for the purpose of having some support by a person of consequence greater than her own, that *she had accepted a marriage proposal from the German soldier she loved beyond all compare, that she must marry if her heart would not be broken and herself consigned to a life of wretchedness, etc. etc. etc.* Despite my efforts to keep the pair of them apart, they had been able to see one another, and he had taken it upon himself to propose. She agreed wholeheartedly, and was fully elated at her prospects.

"So you have been meeting with this gentleman behind my back?" I asked, very discontented by the circumstance which was thus disclos'd to me.

My mother spoke up for her defense. "She has met him without secrecy or impropriety time and again, and if you would take a little more interest in your daughter's life you should have known it yourself."

"I am sorry that you find this so discomfiting," said Charlotte. "It has been no aim of mine to displease you by this action. I have not a single doubt but that you only wish my happiness, my comfort, and the good of the country. I can only throw myself on your goodness and affection for your only child, who I trust you will never attempt to force into a situation that would ensure her misery. You *will* love Leopold once you meet him, I am certain of it. There is no finer gentleman of rank in all of Europe!"

Indeed, his pedigree provided little for me to object about: he was, evidently, the son of the ruling family of Saxe-Coburg-Saalfeld. He had lately been fighting with the Russians in the wars against Napoleon. And when I first saw him, not too long after this event, I was very favourably impressed by his dark hair and fine features. He was,

183

indeed, a lovely man to appear at the side of my daughter. My pride fought me and did not want to allow me to love the fellow, who had so embarrassed and frustrated my designs, but he wore me down, and I relented. Charlotte required my permission to marry, and I at last was prevailed upon to grant her that permission. It was some thing of a humiliation for me to inform the Prince of Orange as to the change in plans, but Charlotte, at least, was overjoyed for her new condition.

The marriage was announc'd to the Privy Council. A suitable house was chosen for the new Royal couple, and a wedding date decided upon. The day before the nuptials, when Leopold went to the house for the first time, he was nearly crushed by the adoring crowds who flock'd to see him.

Exactly twenty one years and twenty four days from the date on which I had been compell'd to marry her mother, Charlotte's own marriage occurred. The wedding itself was held at Carlton House, in the Crimson Drawing Room. The Archbishop of Canterbury conducted. The bride's Royal grandfather was unable to attend, consequent of his health, but the remainder of the family was there. This included Caroline, who had arrived on Charlotte's invitation, and who I somehow had imagined ought to have been too asham'd to shew her face in such a crowd. Yet there she was, with her black-dyed hair and piles of jewelry, smiling vacantly to every body. She was, at this time, briefly returned from the continent upon which she now lived her life to utter contentment. We greeted one another with an icy bow, though despite this minor tension, every body comported themselves well, and the ceremony was completed in harmony and joy for the new couple. As soon as all was finished, Charlotte and her new husband changed their clothes and departed without further ado to their honeymoon.

We the family who were left behind, very naturally fell into an evening of entertainment and celebration. We drank wine, and a supper was put out. Musicians soothed us with a little musick, and those of the party who had a mind to, danced together. I watched with amusement, when Caroline directly walk'd to me and began to speak. In the spirit of the event, we were pleasant to one another.

"Will you not dance?" she asked.

"I think my dancing days have pass'd," I replied. Gout and dropsy had put such strenuous activity as that beyond my abilities. Rusty old creatures we are! Conversation was the only thing open to us, so we conversed over pleasant subjects. I asked her how she was finding the continent; and the answer which she gave was some thing of a surprize to me.

"Oh, it is a delight," she replied. "Every body who is of consequence, lives there now: Lord Byron, Sir Henry Mildmay, Raikes, the Shelleys, Brummell..."

"Beau Brummell is on the continent?" I asked, surpriz'd to learn of that, though I was aware that debtors commonly fled over the sea to escape their obligations.

"Oh, yes," she said. "He lives in Calais. Idle as ever, but his friends send him money enough, and his landlord enjoys his company too well to fault his lack of payment. They call him *le Roi du Calais*, because he is always so well dressed, and lives like a little King out there. Every body knows him."

I was dismayed by this news: I had hop'd to hear that Brummell was ruined and living in squalor, but it sounded as if he was living much as he ever had been, only now in France instead of London.

"Is he in good health?" I asked.

"To all my knowledge," she answered.

That alone meant he did better than I: the pains in my limbs were becoming the bane of my existence. I required laudanum several times a day in order to abide the torment of it. I knew, meanwhile, that Brummell had been infected by the French disease, but evidently he had found adequate treatment to halt the progress of that frightful ailment (at least, enough to disguise it from others.)

"Do you know if Frederica still associates with him?" I asked automatically.

Caroline smirked at that. "Really, you should ask her yourself. He is a little too gallant to discuss his other paramours with me."

My God. My God! She really said that to me! I could not believe it! "You do not mean to convey that you and he…"

She smiled and whispered, "What will you do about it? I am to be back on the boat to-morrow: you will never be able to organize an investigation against me in time; and Brummell is well out of your jurisdiction. Make a fuss about it if you like, but it went on for years enough without any body taking notice till now, and is virtually unprovable at this point."

My heart sank. "I had thought that his interest was directed towards Frederica."

"You know full well that a man can juggle a few different women all at once," she said. "The sweet Beau is always sort of a kept man; and his upkeep is expensive, so he requires a multitude. Surely you knew it yourself, yes?"

I glared at her. The last of my good feeling was gone. "If you are yet again attempting to project upon me whatever erotic interest *you* suffer for Mr. Brummell, I am afraid you have mistaken me, and the nature of my friendship towards him."

She smiled dismissively at my statement. "I do suppose that every one inclines to project their own fears and wishes upon those around them. Perhaps he hates you less than you realize, George: perhaps that was your own idea."

I did not want to make a scene by falling into any great outburst, at this happy event of our daughter's wedding, and so I simply told her, very quietly, to get out of my sight at once. I could not bring myself to speak another word to Caroline for the rest of the night; or ever again, for that matter. Such a revelation was too much for me. She and Brummell, together! I cannot even bear to think of how long this line of conduct must have went on. It is highly probable that she met him during our wedding, for Heaven's sake. I dread to think of all the implications behind it. I cannot consider them: I die at the very idea.

At the end of the night, my family cleared out, and I was left all alone in Carlton House. I sat by the fire, *tutto solo*, sipping my favourite brandy, and reckoning the condition of things.

I had abandoned Isabella by this time; and Maria I am only ever permitted to see in the form of her miniature portrait, dangling from a rotted ribband about my neck. Two wives, and neither one can tolerate me! All my friends have abandon'd me, it seems. I dread to leave the house for fear of being jeered or even ambush'd in the streets, I am so greatly hated. I have had projectiles thrown through the windows of my carriage when proceeding about the city. The people see me as a pretentious glutton, uncaring to their needs, and squandering the wealth of the country on clothes and snuff-boxes. Alas! One may do what one will, to please, and to endeavor to please; yet one can never. *Rex eris, si recte feceris: si non feceris, non eris.*

The name of Brummell is spoken as a byword for a man of fashion. He is now a little older than was I, when I first met him, at Windsor. His situation, in a way, is not too different from what mine had been at the time; but evidently he harboured a bit too much *amour-propre* to marry his way out of debt, and he has resolved his troubles through some other means. I understand Frederica sends plenty of money his way, without condition upon it. I do not know whether Caroline gives him help: I like to imagine he spread his French Disease to her. Perhaps one day he shall find himself like me: old and alone. Yet for now he enjoys himself, with all the others who have escaped me: for that his how greatly I repel them all, that they perceive it as necessary to *escape* from me to some foreign land.

Even my little Charlotte, ultimately, did not stay with me: she died a year after her marriage. Poor heartbroken Leopold return'd to the continent, with every one else.

189

I am alone. I am by myself. I can dress up as much as I like: but what do the clothes matter, when there is nobody to see them? One thing I can say for my condolence: now that I am alone, I can eat all I want. I fret about the cut of my meats the way I once did about the cut of my clothes. There may be no one left to admire my fashions, but neither is there any body to complain about my waistline. I no longer wear that d-----d corset. My body, at least, has been made free from the treacherous grip of Beauty, and from all the sacrifice required to appease that monstrous goddess. In fact, with my father out of his senses, the dandies destroyed, and my lovers forsaken, I might truly say that my circumstances have never look'd better. I am able to do as I please, without judgment. Venus is the goddess of Love and of Beauty, but she also rules over Musick: and for now, my cello is quite enough company for my tastes. Beauty is too fragile a virtue for pursuit.

***

END.

AUTHOR'S NOTES.

A. Aspinall's collected *Letters of King George IV* were consulted in order to imitate the writing style of George IV/The Prince Regent/Prinny, and to mimic his personality as nearly as my capability would allow for. Prinny's spelling habits were shown to be very inconsistent, probably due to the flexibility of writing rules at the time, and perhaps dependent upon whether he was being assisted in his writing by a secretary, colleague, etc. as it is evident was sometimes the case. At times he uses spellings which are nowadays considered to be Americanisms (e.g. *color*, *honor*) as well as some spellings which are merely old-fashioned (e.g. *risque* for risk, *idiotick* for idiotic.) The original letters also include a good share of simple misspellings (e.g. *atchieve* for achieve, *dispair* for despair) which I decided against imitating for fear that readers would merely mistake it for poor copyediting on my part. 18th and early 19th century punctuation was modeled less on rules of syntax than it was on making sentences "sound" right on the page, and I've followed that in imitation of Prinny's stylings.

Prinny also displayed a tendency to spontaneously slip into French, or less often Latin or Italian. German words tended to appear in his vocabulary only when speaking of appropriately German topics.

Perhaps the most difficult of his habits to decode was the use of apostrophes to designate the omission of sounds which modern English does not include in the first place, and which were dropped commonly enough already that most other authors of his era did not use them — we speak of course of words like *appriz'd, receiv'd, wou'd, cou'd, altho'*. He seems to have been more likely to use these designations in his less formal letters, but his decision-making process is not too apparent. I was left to decide upon my own set of rules for applying them.

As with almost any work of historical fiction, some artistic license has been taken. My most frequent crime against the historical record was to fudge the dates at which certain events took place — for instance, Brummell's flight from London occurred on May 16th, 1816, a couple weeks *after* Charlotte's wedding on May 2nd of that year. One who catches these errors might be permitted to suppose that Prinny is simply misremembering the details in his personal recollection of the events. More blatant violations of the record include Caroline's presence at her daughter's wedding (she was not there) and some like adjustments done to enhance the dramatic flow. A decided effort was made to imply that Charlotte's German soldier, who was sent away to Spain, was the same German soldier that she eventually married: these were, in actuality, two different men.

Several books and websites provided educational material used for the research that went into this story, the most notable being Captain Jesse's *Life of George Brummell, Esq., Commonly Called Beau Brummell,* James Munson's *Maria Fitzherbert: The Secret Wife of George IV,* and the websites The Regency Encyclopedia and Dandyism.net. A nod should also be given to Etymonline.com for easing along my efforts to use only period-correct language.

Printed in Great Britain
by Amazon

82945658R00119